out of balance

A Novel

angela lam turpin

iUniverse, Inc.
Bloomington

Copyright © 2011 by Angela Lam Turpin

All rights reserved. No part of this book may be used or reproduced by any means, graphic, electronic, or mechanical, including photocopying, recording, taping or by any information storage retrieval system without the written permission of the publisher except in the case of brief quotations embodied in critical articles and reviews.

iUniverse books may be ordered through booksellers or by contacting:

iUniverse
1663 Liberty Drive
Bloomington, IN 47403
www.iuniverse.com
1-800-Authors (1-800-288-4677)

Because of the dynamic nature of the Internet, any web addresses or links contained in this book may have changed since publication and may no longer be valid. The views expressed in this work are solely those of the author and do not necessarily reflect the views of the publisher, and the publisher hereby disclaims any responsibility for them.

Any people depicted in stock imagery provided by Thinkstock are models, and such images are being used for illustrative purposes only.

Certain stock imagery © Thinkstock.

ISBN: 978-1-4502-9438-6 (sc)
ISBN: 978-1-4502-9440-9 (hc)
ISBN: 978-1-4502-9439-3 (ebook)

Printed in the United States of America

iUniverse rev. date: 03/24/2011

Once again

For Ed

Acknowledgments

Thanks to my first readers, especially my husband, Ed, who always manages to find a way to make things better. Thanks to Sylvia Lam for the author photograph. Thanks to Foery K. MacDonnell for editing. Thanks to Scott Weiss for asking the right questions to get the right answers for the creation of the back cover copy. Thanks to Carol Taylor-Lueck at Best Wishes for carrying my books and greeting cards. Carol's dedication to local artists is what makes shopping local, shopping better. Thanks to my husband who sacrificed sleep, guitar practice, late night runs, and a much needed haircut to magically transform my website at www.angelalamturpin.com. Thanks to my son, Gabriel, for inspiring Frank's love of music, and to my daughter, Rose, for brainstorming with me. And a special thank you to all of my fans who kept encouraging me to write another book.

Chapter 1

Every morning, Franklin Benjamin Martin, the President and CEO of Vine Valley Bank, swaggers into the bank's administrative office dressed in a white T-shirt, gray linen blazer, and tight jeans. He wears his black aviator sunglasses on the top of his salt and pepper hair and whistles, "Highway to Hell." I sit at the front desk, doodling in my sketchbook. Frank slaps a drum roll on the counter and asks, "How's it going, babe?"

"Just fine." I close my sketchbook and nudge it under a stack of Bank Security Act reports. I grab the button advertising Vine Valley's motto, "Bank Better," and reluctantly fasten it above my heart.

But Frank does not seem to care whether I am drawing or filing. He crosses his arms on the high counter and leans toward me with a seductively crooked smile. The skin crinkles around his hazel eyes. He smells like the ocean. God, how I wish it was summer and I was at the beach painting a portrait of my husband, Eric, playing in the waves with our eight-year-old daughter, Zenith. Since I started working at Vine Valley Bank, it seems like all I do is sit at this desk directing phone calls and filing. How I miss being a stay-at-home mom. All those free hours with my family traded for a paycheck.

"How fast can you type?" Frank asks.

"Umm. Eighty words a minute," I say. It's a lie. I've never been tested.

He purses his lips and nods, as if listening to an invisible rock band playing in his mind. "Not bad. Do you get sick on long car rides on windy roads?"

Where is this conversation going? "No, sir," I say. "Do you?"

But he does not answer my question. "How about coming with me to World Bank in Spa County? I have a meeting and Emilio's on vacation. I need someone to take notes. If we leave now, we'll be back by five so you can go home on time, okay?"

What do I know about corporate meetings and dictation? I stuff envelopes and answer phones. Doesn't Frank know this? I fiddle with the papers on my desk, hoping the phone will ring and rescue me from answering his question. But the switchboard is dark and lifeless. I think about sitting in a room full of bankers, trying to focus on the conversation long enough to type everything down, word for word. My stomach clenches. I lift my head and meet Frank's expectant gaze. There is something in those hazel eyes that I have never seen in anyone here at the bank—trust. Frank trusts that I can do the job. Plus, I'll be out of the office, driving around in Frank's trendy new Porsche, and enjoying the view of vineyards and country mansions as we speed along the back roads. Enthusiasm starts to build in my chest. Maybe I can sketch a few ideas for a new landscape. My fingers twitch with excitement. Still, I ask, "Who will answer the phones if I'm gone?"

Frank reaches down and buzzes Jim, the HR manager who hired me three months ago.

"Yes, Bev?" Jim says, thinking it's me.

"I'm borrowing the receptionist for the day," Frank says, in a loud, authoritative voice. "Can you watch the phones?"

Jim rushes out of his office. He's a fat man with stubby legs. I instinctively raise my hand to cover my chest although I'm wearing a very professional scooped neck blouse. Why didn't Eric throw a few of my baggy turtleneck sweaters into the washer yesterday when he was getting the grass stains out of Zenith's soccer uniform? It would have only taken a moment, right? Now I'm stuck with Jim narrowing his gaze at my chest and asking, "Where are you two going?" like he's an overprotective parent.

Frank motions for me to gather my belongings. I grab my purse and tuck the sketchbook under my arm. Frank places his hand on my shoulder and guides me toward the double glass doors. "We're going to take over the World," Frank says, winking. "World Bank, that is."

The soft buttery seats in Frank's new Porsche hug my back. The entire car smells of new leather. Mmm. I love that smell. It's something I only get to sniff when I'm out window shopping for purses, because without Eric working, I can't afford to splurge on anything new. Okay, I can buy $1.99 nylons found at the supermarket, but only because it's a work expense. I stretch out my legs and open my sketchbook in my lap and twirl the pencil between my fingers. The first signs of Fall have given the air a bitter chill, and Frank blasts the heater to warm us up a bit. When the car is a comfortable temperature, he turns the heater off and turns on the MP3 player hooked up to his stereo. Metallica plays "Enter Sandman."

Frank drives fast. He catches me staring at his hands and feet, shifting gears and steering expertly through traffic. "I took a few classes at Infineon," he explains. "I always wanted to be Mario Andretti, but I couldn't convince my dad it was more important than running. He was a track star and he thought I should be one like him, but I've always preferred driving to running. How about you?"

I shrug. "I don't care for either one."

"You prefer writing instead?" he asks, nodding toward my sketchbook.

I place my hand over the paper instinctively trying to cover it up, although the page is blank. "Actually, I'm an aspiring artist."

"Aspiring? What's that supposed to mean?"

I remember the conversation I had at the kitchen table last Thanksgiving when I mentioned I was content to paint and care for Zenith, although Eric had been out of work and his unemployment had run out. My mother politely asked when I was going to get a real job, since I hadn't made any money being an aspiring artist.

"Artists make money," I explain. "Aspiring artists don't."

Frank guffaws. "Who told you that hogwash? And more importantly, why do you believe it?"

My face burns with embarrassment. "I don't have any formal training."

"And you think I do as the bank's president?" he asks. "Seriously, Bev, you're got some learning to do. And I don't mean book learning either." He turns onto the freeway and speeds over to the fast lane. I can't see his eyes behind his sunglasses, but his mouth twitches like he's trying to stop himself from saying something he might regret. "I didn't go to college either, and I didn't let that stop me from getting where I am. It's all about knowing how to learn and who to learn it from. When I started with the bank, I was just a loan officer, trying to get by on a few loans a month. But I met a really interesting guy, Stewart McGill, and he taught me everything I needed to know about how to talk to the big guys and make them switch accounts. Within months, I was the top loan officer in the bank. Then, when the chief credit officer retired, I applied for his position. I wasn't the most qualified or experienced, but I got the job because of tenacity and hard work."

I stare down at the blank sheet of paper and think of all the paintings lining the back of the bedroom closet next to last season's shoes. Maybe I should hang a few up in the house and proudly display my meek efforts.

"What type of art do you do?" Frank asks.

"Acrylic painting," I say. "I started when Zenith was a toddler learning how to finger paint. It was so much fun. The paint is water-based and dries quickly, so it's easy to cart around when you're a busy mom."

"Have you approached any galleries?"

I laugh. Galleries? Who is he kidding?

"Seriously, Bev, you can't get anywhere if you just paint for fun. You have to take a risk, expose yourself. Or you'll always be aspiring." He snickers at his own joke.

I close the sketchbook and set it beside my feet. Why would I want to expose myself for the world to judge? My gaze drifts out the window at the passing cars. I wonder what Eric is doing while Zenith is in school. Shopping for dinner? I hate the way Eric shops, hustling down each aisle with his list, checking off each item as he places it in the cart, and keeping a running total in his head. But I'm stuck here, in this car, far from any stores. I've heard Spa County has lots of tiny shops full of unique knick-knacks. Hmm. Maybe we'll have time to stop and look a bit. Wouldn't that make the whole trip worth it? Getting paid to window shop. Now that's my kind of job.

I lean back against the soft leather seat and watch Frank slap the steering wheel in time with the drum solo. "Why don't you tell me more about this visit to World Bank," I say, shifting the focus back to work.

The merriment drains from his face. "What I have to say is confidential. Only the Board of Directors knows the reason for this visit." He turns down the volume on AC/DC's "Big Balls" and lowers his voice. "A few months ago, I was notified by a little birdie that World Bank was having some problems with their loan portfolio. I approached their president with an offer to buy up some of their troubled loans, but he brushed me off, saying the bank was fine. They didn't want to sell anything. Three months later, he calls me back and invites me to lunch to discuss some issues, which is the purpose of our visit today."

Discuss some issues? "What do you think he wants to discuss?"

Frank slaps the steering wheel to the beat of the drum. "I think World Bank might be in over their heads with the Fed and they want us to bail them out before the FDIC takes them over."

Wow. A hostile takeover. Right in our backyard. "That can happen?" I ask.

Frank flashes that seductively crooked smile. "This is banking, babe. Anything can happen."

Chapter 2

We arrive at the Warm Water Restaurant and Hotel fifteen minutes before our appointment. A valet parks the Porsche. I slip my sketchbook into my purse and Frank hands me a leather laptop bag that looks more like a sleek briefcase and feels more like a bowling ball. The heat of early October feels more like the thick of summer in Spa County, and I fear the beads of sweat against the nape of my neck might release a trickle of moisture down my spine.

We climb the brief flight of stairs and a doorman opens the gold-framed glass door of the hotel. The concierge at the front desk directs us to the restaurant at the end of the marble-floored, glass-domed foyer. A canopy of plants creates an exotic atmosphere at the entrance, and for a moment, I wonder if I might glimpse a celebrity. *People* magazine reported that Geena Davis had her reception dinner at the Warm Water Restaurant and Hotel, and although that was several years ago, who's to say Lady Gaga won't stop by for a visit before heading to Finland for the European leg of her tour?

"Nervous?" Frank asks, while we wait to be seated.

I shift the laptop bag to my other hand and run my fingers through my hair. My stomach feels fine, although my legs seem a little bit wobbly from the pair of spiky heels I decided to wear. But my throat is dry. And my mind is wandering just a tad. "Fine," I say. "I'm absolutely fine, although I'll probably need to freshen up a bit after we're shown to our table."

"Why don't you go now? I'll even watch the laptop. Restrooms are behind us to the right."

I hand him the bag and escape into the plush red velvet powder room. It feels like the back stage of an old theater with its gilded mirrors and big bulbous lights on the walls. My heels click clack over the expensive Italian tiles. White shutters act as doors on the stalls. My mother used to say you can always tell the quality of a restaurant from the condition of the bathroom. I'd have to say this place must be five stars. There are even tiny decorative soaps next to the three sinks on the marble counters and both the hot and cold water in the faucet work. I grab a paper towel and moisten it to dab the sweat from my forehead and the nape of my neck. The skin around my eyes looks tired and the frown lines around my mouth have deepened. I wish I had the time and the money to get a facial while we are here. Wouldn't it be great to have plump, youthful skin without the pimples? Isn't that what everyone looks forward to when they grow up? No one tells you marriage and childrearing and work take a bigger toll on your skin than tanning and forgetting to use daily moisturizer and eating the wrong food combinations. None of the beauty magazines report any of those issues. If they did, no one would want to get married and have children or pursue a career, and surely the working population of the United States would plunge as quickly as the illegal immigrant population rises. We would become a nation of handouts until there was nothing left to handout.

Like the bank bailout, I think. From what I know, Vine Valley Bank did not take any bailout money because they did not need the funds, but several local banks did, such as World Bank, and they are still in trouble according to what Frank implied during our drive.

I rejoin Frank at the entrance to the restaurant. He has placed his sunglasses on the top of his head. His gaze meets my gaze, never once traveling up and down the curves of my body. It's strange and refreshing, almost like having lunch with a girlfriend. A girlfriend dressed like a rock star and armed with intimate knowledge of the financial world.

A waiter in a crisp tuxedo directs us to a table near the floor-to-ceiling windows overlooking the rows of quaint shops lining the street. I take a seat and Frank sits next to me, leaving the space directly across from me available for the president of World Bank.

Frank orders a round of soda. "I'm not one to drink while doing business," he explains.

"Shall I open the laptop and get ready to take notes?" I ask.

Frank shakes his head. "Not unless he wants to start negotiating. You can use your notebook till then."

I remove my sketchbook and start to draw the view of the street with the tourists in their wide-brimmed hats, big sunglasses, and Capri pants. I sketch the storefront windows of the stationery store, the vases and bowls in the ceramics shop, and the line of customers leading into the café. Frank leans toward me, silently observing my work. Usually, I am self-conscious about my drawing unless I'm around children, because children don't care about talent. They just appreciate you for who you are. But Frank's gaze seems as innocent as a child.

My sketchbook is my diary. It captures important moments in my life. This is the first time I've been to a luxurious restaurant on business and it may be my last. I want to remember this moment, sitting on an antique chair with a view of Main Street, with the bank's President beside me just moments before negotiations begin.

I turn to a blank page when the waiter returns with our drinks. An older gentleman in a smart suit approaches our table. Frank stands up and introduces us. "Buddy Levert, this is Beverly Mael, my Executive Assistant."

Executive Assistant sounds much classier than Receptionist. I stand up and shake Buddy's meaty hand. His gaze rests a few inches below my eyes. He's shorter than Frank by a foot, but taller than me. He has a round face with beady black eyes, and skin speckled with age spots. He's bald and his belly is much larger than his chest. He looks like a distinguished penguin.

After we place our orders—steak and fries for Buddy, salmon and grilled vegetables for Frank, and a lobster salad for me—Buddy and Frank talk about golf and the upcoming Harvest Fair. Buddy nods and smiles at me, although he is talking to Frank. I stare down at my silverware and twirl my napkin in my lap. In a few weeks it will be Halloween. I wonder if everyone dresses up at the bank and if they do, whether or not I can find time to make a costume.

I know we can't afford to purchase anything. Even though Eric has been clipping coupons and selling junk in our garage on eBay, the money will go toward Zenith and Eric's costumes, since they will be attending the classroom's annual Halloween party, not me. What if everyone in the bank does dress up? What do I have that I can wear? Last year I was Marilyn Monroe. I really don't want to wear that to the bank with Jim sitting in the office beside me. He will find an excuse to walk by every other minute to see if he can get a peek at my breasts. Oh, well. Maybe Eric will earn enough from selling our junk so I can buy a costume too.

"So tell me what prompted this meeting?" asks Frank.

I perk up and grab my pencil, ready to take notes.

Buddy hiccups from swallowing too much of his soda too quickly. He pats his lips with a napkin, leans back against his chair, and says, "I'm proposing a merger. With your assets and World's name, we can take over the banking industry in Northern California. We'd be bigger and better than the nationals, because our devotion to the community is stronger, and our commitment to local lending is better than ever."

The waiter brings our entrees. I close my sketchbook and tuck it into my purse. Buddy cuts into his steak. Frank doesn't touch his salmon. He watches Buddy eat with as much interest as one might watch a tiger feeding at the zoo. I wonder what Frank's thinking, but I'm too afraid to ask. I spear my lettuce. Mmm. Is that lemon in the dressing? Buddy continues to stare at me. And I gaze at Frank, thankful that he's sitting beside me. Otherwise, Buddy might think this is some sort of date, not a business meeting.

Frank places his arms on the table, one on each side of his plate, and gazes directly at Buddy, although Buddy is still looking at me. "You should have sold those loans to us when we offered," Frank says. "Now you have to worry about how you're going to look once your audit is made public."

Buddy chokes on his steak. He reaches for his glass of water and takes a few gulps. His eyes are glassy and red. "How do you know about our audit?"

Frank flashes his crooked smile. "A little birdie told me."

"Who?"

Frank refuses to answer. He takes a bite of his salmon and nods. "The food here is to die for, isn't it?"

I chew on the tender lobster and crisp lettuce and nod.

Buddy turns his focus away from me and directs it to Frank. "When I find out who told you confidential information—"

"It'll be too late. The government will seize you. You'll become another casualty of the subprime meltdown." Frank lowers his voice conspiratorially. "Unless you let us help you."

Buddy's gaze rests on my chest and his breathing quickens. "What are you proposing?"

"We buy you out at a fraction of your worth."

"How much?"

"Twenty-five cents for every dollar."

"Impossible. The Board will never approve it."

Frank shrugs. "I guess that's one way to make front page news."

Buddy purses his lips. "Okay. I'll bring it to the Board at the end of the month. But I can't promise you they'll take it. They may want to counter."

"No problem." Frank bends down and removes a stack of papers from the laptop bag. "Here's the formal proposal, approved by my Board. I look forward to hearing from you at the end of the month."

After lunch, Frank slips his sunglasses over his eyes, grabs my hand, and leads me across the street. My gait picks up to a trot. Shopping, here we come! But Frank dips into the café.

"You're still hungry?" I'm dizzy from the thick scent of coffee and pastries.

Frank places his sunglasses on top of his head. "I've got to get my caffeine fix. My wife hates it, but I just can't go without three mochas a day."

"Three?"

He nods. "My wife's a health nut. I've adopted organic cooking, meditation, yoga, and alternative medicine to keep the peace, but I won't give up chocolate or coffee."

While Frank stands in line, I wander around the café. The blond wood-paneled walls are covered with original paintings from local artists. I stop in front of a painting depicting the view from the restaurant across the street. It's just like my sketch, only better, with rich autumnal colors painted in broad strokes. The painting captures the welcoming warmth of small town life.

"Hey, didn't you just draw that?" Frank asks, sipping his mocha.

"I *wish* that was my painting," I say.

I continue to gaze in admiration of the artist's brushwork. Frank stands reverently beside me. It feels like a moment of worship.

Frank finishes his mocha. "The lobby could use a painting, don't you think?"

The walls of Vine Valley Bank are chalk white and bare, except for the double glass doors and the wide windows overlooking the parking lot.

"It is kind of uninspiring." I've often thought of painting the walls a honey color and bringing in a few plants and a couple of mirrors for a bit of feng shui. But a painting would do the trick, too. The sticker next to the painting reads, "Scene from Warm Water Restaurant, an original acrylic painting by V.S. for $1,200." I gape at the price. No way could I afford $1,200 for a painting. That's more than our mortgage payment each month.

But Frank is undaunted. He goes to the counter and pays for the painting with the bank's VISA.

"I can't believe you bought that," I stammer.

"Why not?" Frank slips his sunglasses over his eyes and tucks the painting under one arm. "Everyone deserves a little inspiration."

Chapter 3

I walk through the door of our two bedroom house to see Eric sitting at the computer in the living room typing furiously. His broad back faces me. I slip off my heels, set my purse on the coffee table, and plant a kiss on his bald head.

"Zenith finished her homework early," Eric says, still typing. "She's in the backyard playing with Mindi. Vi had an evening client and her sitter canceled. I hope you don't mind."

"No, of course not." Vi Patel has been my friend since we met in a Mommy and Me yoga class when our girls were infants. She's a marriage and family psychologist and a single parent since her husband, Bob, left her for an older woman two years ago.

Eric stops typing and pivots in his chair. "Hope you don't mind, but I'm working on this metasploit. I'd like to test it this weekend."

Eric loves computers. He used to work for a big corporation making big money fixing their network, until the IT manager discovered Eric performing unauthorized activities. The first time it happened, Eric was warned. We decided to buy a smaller house and pay a larger down payment. The second time it happened, Eric was demoted with a severe cut in pay. We had to apply for a scholarship for Zenith to continue at the private school she attends. The third time it happened, Eric was laid-off with a modest severance package. We tightened our budget and lived off our savings until the money ran out. That's when I had to get a job. Sometimes I wish Eric had not been dismissed. Sure, he's a lovable guy, but he's also a perpetual prankster. He swears he was not hacking, but I know he's lying. How else do you explain trying to break into your company's network with a homemade script?

I really don't mind whether Eric writes code to protect the Pentagon or Macy's credit card database. I just sometimes wish he had not been caught. It would have simplified our lives.

"Dinner's almost ready," Eric says, pulling me into his lap. "How was your day?"

I grin with delight. "The President took me with him to Spa County for a business lunch."

"Really?" Eric's strong arms tighten against me. "Why would he do that?"

"Frank's assistant is on vacation and he needed me to take notes."

The buzzer rings in the kitchen. Eric lifts me up and carries me across the living room. Since he's been unemployed, he's been working out every day in our neighbor's garage gym with their teenage son who plays on Vine Valley High School's football team. Eric's much stronger than when I met him fifteen years ago. Back then, he was a straggly college student with a Mountain Dew addiction that he kept fueled with trips to my father's corner grocery store where I worked. The mothers of Zenith's classmates think he's a professional body builder.

He sets me down near the sink and pulls the roasted chicken out of the oven. It smells of garlic and rosemary and thyme. Mmm. Eric's also a better chef than me. I hate to admit it, but being a full-time husband and father really suits him.

I get the dishes and set the table, remembering the day. "We went to this really nice restaurant, and I sketched the view across the street while waiting for the President of World Bank to arrive. Before we left, we saw the same view painted by a local artist. And guess what? Frank bought it for the bank. And it cost twelve hundred dollars!"

Eric frowns as he cuts the chicken. "What a waste of corporate funds!"

"But Frank said we needed a painting in the lobby. It was an investment."

"And what was Frank's meeting about?"

"Oh, he wants to buy World Bank for pennies on the dollar."

"And you have notes on that?"

I shrug.

"Ah, I see." Eric sets the carved chicken on the table. "You were there for eye candy."

Eye candy? Is that all Eric thinks about my employable skills? That I'm some pretty face to help close some big deal?

Well, Buddy *did* keep staring at me even when he was talking to Frank. But still.

"I had the company's laptop for taking notes," I say in my defense.

"Did you use it?"

Well, not really. I was too busy sketching, but I don't want to tell Eric that. "Of course," I lie. "I'd show you my notes, but the laptop is at the bank. Frank won't let me take it home. Bank security, you know."

Eric nods. "I bet I could penetrate their network with this new metasploit I'm working on."

"You wouldn't."

"I could." He grins mischievously.

"Don't. You promised you would be good."

"I *am* good. I'm going to save the world from terrorists breaking into the bank and wiring funds into their accounts."

I do not doubt Eric's skill, only his intention. He's such a joker. Like when he ran the virus killing mechanism on my parents' computer. When it was done cleaning their system, a clown tap danced across their monitor singing songs from *The Sound of Music*. Eric's a big kid with a big weapon, and sometimes I don't know how he's going to use it. I could just see a teller trying to withdraw money from a customer's account, only to receive the error, *Insufficient funds*, followed by *Gotcha sucker*, and the account's true balance displayed in flashing neon green numbers.

The back door opens and Zenith and Mindi tumble inside. Zenith pushes the brown curls off her forehead with the back of her muddy hand. Her cheeks are almost as brown as Mindi's skin.

Mindi's long black hair is tied in a low pony tail. Mud is speckled on her jeans. Without a word, the girls wash their hands in the kitchen sink and sit down at opposite sides of the table.

"Hello, Mrs. Mael," Mindi says. "How are you?"

"Fine, thanks," I say, remembering how Vi likes to teach her daughter manners. "And you?"

"Very well. Thank you for asking."

Zenith smiles up at me. "I'm well, too, Mommy. Daddy corrected my math, and Mindi and I are building mud castles next to the garden."

I take a seat at the head of the table across from Eric. We all make the Sign of the Cross and say grace. Even though Vi practices Buddhism, Bob goes to our church. So Mindi gets to be part of two religions, which must be pretty confusing, if you ask me. But Mindi doesn't seem to mind. I guess that's one of the perks of having a psychologist for a mother.

Dinner goes well. There's plenty of roasted chicken, steamed carrots and broccoli, and enough brown rice to keep us fed for the week. Just four months ago, we were eating peanut butter and jelly sandwiches three times a day. We cut cable, discontinued COBRA, applied for food stamps, and biked everywhere. Now we can afford TV. The bank pays for our health insurance. We shop at Groceries for Less. Eric drives Zenith to school, but I bike to work most days. We have chosen to rebuild our savings account rather than splurge on luxuries like manicures and pedicures, season tickets to the Sharks games, art and music lessons, and weekend getaways.

I glance around the table, admiring my family and my friend's daughter.

Life is good.

Vi arrives after we've finished putting leftovers away and loading the dishwasher. Her black hair has been cut into a short bob and falls against her brown chin in a stylish wave. She shares her daughter's black eyes and glow-in-the-dark smile. Is that the new Chanel perfume I smell on her?

"Hey, Bev, how's work?" Vi asks.

I eye Vi's new Gucci handbag. God, it looks so much better than the picture in *Vogue* that I saw in the break room. I almost want to ask where she bought it, how much it cost, and do they have any left, but I know I can't afford to even daydream.

Eric strolls into the living room and spoils my news. "Bev went with the bank's President on a business lunch."

Vi gives me the *Real Housewives* once over: hair, outfit, shoes. Her gaze stops at my breasts. "They must have been negotiating a big deal," Vi says, "to bring in the big guns."

Eric laughs.

I flush slightly, clenching my hands at my sides. Why do they both think my only asset is my chest?

"I happen to be part of the team negotiating the takeover of World Bank," I say, trying to make myself sound more important than I feel. "And I took notes on the company laptop."

Vi smiles patronizingly and gathers Mindi. Before she leaves, Vi solemnly says, "I think that's great you're being promoted from the front desk. Are you getting a raise?"

I wish. Maybe I shouldn't have said anything. Now she'll think we can spend weekends together shopping at Neiman Marcus. And I can't.

"Not yet," I say. "It all depends on whether or not this deal goes through."

"Well, good luck," Vi says.

Thanks, I think, closing the front door. I'll need it.

Chapter 4

When I arrive at the bank the next morning, the painting Frank purchased hangs in the lobby above the two plush leather chairs facing the entrance to the conference room. I set my purse underneath the front desk and head into the break room to brew two pots of coffee—one regular, one decaf.

The women from the accounting department swarm like harpies around the pink pastry box on the table. I try to ignore them as I start the coffee, but their voices carry.

"We got all these numbers from World Bank, and I don't know what we're supposed to do with them," Tina says, between bites of a glazed donut.

"It's probably just another loan participation," Kim says, licking the sugar off her fingertips.

"Then why would he bring the receptionist with him?" Lorraine asks.

"It must be something big if he wants to distract them," Tina says. "Do you think they're negotiating a merger?"

"I bet that old man at World would agree to anything once he took a look at that rack," Kim says.

They burst into giggles. I switch pots, accidentally clanging the glass carafe against the counter. They glance up from their huddle and finally notice me.

"Hi, Bev," Tina says, flashing a false smile. "How are you doing this morning?"

"Just peachy," I say, trying to keep my voice steady. My hands shake as I start to brew the second pot. My knees feel weak. I try to pour myself a cup of coffee, but it splashes on the counter. I silently curse, grab some paper towels, and mop up the mess.

The women gawk at me like I'm an exotic creature at the zoo. Eric managed to wash my favorite loose-fitting, high-neck blouse, and I'm wearing the bra that promises to minimize my chest, but I can still tell they are staring at my only asset.

Forgoing the coffee, I stride out of the break room, blinking fast to stem the threat of tears.

At a quarter to eleven, Frank strides into the lobby whistling, "Love in an Elevator." I transfer the caller to New Accounts and hang up the line. Our eyes meet for a brief second, and Frank flashes his crooked smile. "Hey, babe, I have a project for you." He slaps a stack of papers on the counter. "I need these accounts reconciled and neither Loan Servicing nor Accounting can find the error."

I glance away and swallow. "But—I—don't—know accounting."

Frank crosses his arms on the counter and leans forward conspiratorially. "Do you know how to balance your checkbook?"

"Of course." I always know exactly how much I have in the joint checking account, which is $39.45 until payday on Friday.

"Then you can do this. It's the same thing, only the numbers are a little bigger."

I pick up the sheets of paper and start to browse through them. "How much is the account off by?"

"These numbers are from World Bank. They are missing $2 million. Find it and lunch is on me today. Got it?"

Something swells inside my chest. I grab the calculator underneath my sketchbook and turn it on.

Frank points his fingers at me like they're double barreled guns and slowly backs up toward the double glass doors. "I'm counting on you, babe."

And even though my stomach clenches in fear over the challenge, a smile spreads across my face.

***

An hour later, I find the error. Actually, it's a series of errors, where the credits were put into the debit column and the debits just kept mounting up until the bank was shown owing $2 million it didn't actually owe.

Goodness knows where those credits should have been applied. I can't seem to find the key code that defines the general ledger accounts. All I know is that the accounts from 57000 through 62000 are missing numbers.

I phone Frank with the news.

"Great job, Bev! I'm going to give your findings to the bank's Controller and have her sort it out with her staff." In the background, Bon Jovi sings, "You Give Love a Bad Name." I imagine Frank leaning back in his leather executive chair with his sunglasses propped on the top of his head. "So, tell me, where do you want to go for lunch? Chateau Bistro? Bella Marie?"

"Katz Koffee," I say. It's been over a year since I've tasted one of their hot pastrami on rye sandwiches. I can almost smell the fresh bread baking in the kitchen.

"Are you sure?" Frank asks. "The bank's paying."

"Would you rather go someplace else?" I ask, feeling uncouth and vulgar at the suggestion of a pedestrian café.

Frank pauses. "You know, they have the best mochas in town."

Katz Koffee is crowded. We stand in the lobby and wait for the hostess to call us. People glance at Frank, then at me. I shift from foot to foot and wonder if I cross my arms over my breasts, will that bring more attention to them? Frank does not seem to notice the stares we get. Men and women give me the once over, before staring at Frank, who stands against the wall with his sunglasses propped on the top of his head, humming, "Bad Company."

By the time the waitress calls us, I don't feel like eating. I want to go home, curl up under the covers, and fall asleep for 100 years. But then some prince would come by and stare at my chest and decide to kiss me, and I'd have to deal with reality again.

The waitress leads us to a booth by the kitchen. I slide across the leather seat and smell roast beef and coffee. My stomach growls. Maybe I'm hungrier than I want to admit.

Frank opens the menu and starts to read the items. "What are you having?"

"Pastrami on rye."

"Sounds good." He closes the menu and folds his arms on the table.

"Buddy called today. He wanted to know what we thought of the information he sent. I didn't tell him about the $2 million error. I just told him we're still looking over the numbers."

I sip from my glass of iced water. "How did you know World Bank was in trouble?"

Frank leans forward and whispers, "Sometimes it pays to listen to gossip."

I remember the women in the break room tittering about my breasts. I flush with fresh humiliation.

"What's wrong?" Frank asks.

I shrug. How do you tell your boss the women in Accounting are talking about your breasts?

"I don't like gossip."

Frank taps his fingers on the table. "Neither do I. Most of it is trivial and senseless. But every now and then, you overhear something you won't read about in a sanitized press release. That's what I'm after. The hidden truth."

A waitress takes our order. After she leaves, Frank says, "I have a feeling something's going on that World Bank doesn't want the public to know about. I just haven't been able to put my finger on it yet."

Hmm. I wonder if it is insider trading, money laundering, or international espionage.

"What do you think it is?" I ask.

Frank shrugs. "Your guess is as good as mine."

Chapter 5

When I arrive home that evening, Zenith sits at the kitchen table going over her homework with Eric. I set my purse on the counter and slip off my heels and undo the butterfly clip holding up my hair.

Zenith nibbles on the end of her eraser while Eric tries to explain the concept of multiplication. But every time Eric says something like "integers" and "whole numbers" and "positive number," Zenith's brown eyes glaze over and her teeth gnaw on the rubber until there is nothing left of her eraser.

"Honey, why don't I try to help her?" I place my hand on Eric's shoulder. He glances up at me and frowns.

"I have a minor in mathematics," he says, as if that answers the question.

But Zenith tosses her pencil on the table and looks up at me with exasperation. "Mommy used to help me all the time. I want her to do it, Daddy."

Eric sighs. "Fine. I'll go make some dinner." He brushes past me without a kiss, and I sink down onto the chair next to my daughter and run my fingers through her curls.

"Let's see," I say, examining the page of questions. "Oh, so you're learning just the concept today."

"It's really hard," Zenith says. "You have that big X between the numbers. It looks like two swords fighting."

I bite my lower lip to keep from smiling. "It's not that scary," I tell her. "Multiplication is just a shortcut for adding. Like when you and Mindi take the alley between our neighbors' homes to get to the park. You save time. Look. When you multiply 2 X 3, you are really adding the number 2 three times in a row. 2+2+2 equals?"

Zenith stares at the page. "Six!"

"That's right." I kiss the top of her head. "You're brilliant."

"Let me try." She picks up her pencil and pulls the paper close to her.

I head down the hallway to my bedroom and change into jeans and an oversized T-shirt.

Zenith is halfway done with her homework by the time I return to the kitchen. Eric stands at the stove stirring a pot of boiling water. "What are we having?" I ask, kissing the back of his head.

He harrumphs and pulls away. "I tried telling her what you told her, but she wouldn't listen."

I can't believe he's hurt because our daughter doesn't understand his explanation of how multiplication works. "You used big words," I say. "She's only eight."

Eric stops stirring, turns down the heat, and empties a bag of noodles into the pot. "I don't appreciate how you waltzed in like a superhero saving the day."

A superhero? That's what he thinks I'm trying to be? "She was frustrated. If I didn't say something, she would have started to cry."

Eric shakes the wooden spoon at me. "How is she supposed to learn about real life if you keep coddling her?"

"Hush." I glance over my shoulder. Zenith's head is downcast and her pencil moves across the paper. "I don't want our daughter to hear us arguing."

Eric sets the spoon down and points at the door to the backyard. "Should we go outside and handle this like adults?"

Does he want to fist fight? With me? Surely, he can't be serious. I'm his wife, not a bully. Has staying home made him regress into a teenager? I think back, trying to remember if I was ever this immature when I was a stay-at-home mom. I shudder, recalling nights when Eric came home and I blathered on and on like a whiny woman. I wanted more help around the house, more spontaneous romance, and more extravagant trips than we could afford, because the housewives on the hill always talked about their full-time housekeepers and nannies, their weekly bouquets with handwritten love poems written by their husbands, and their weekend getaways to Paris.

Maybe Eric spends too much time with Brody lifting weights and talking about fist fights. He needs to get out with other fathers and discuss politics and religion. Surely, there's a father's group he can go to. Hmm. Maybe I'll ask Vi how to approach the topic without throwing up any red flags. She's an expert on things like this, isn't she? Doesn't matter that her own marriage fell apart. People pay her $125 an hour to tell them what they need to do to fix theirs. But what can I say now to put an end to this silly argument? Apologize? For what? I lower my voice. "I was just trying to help."

"Go make a salad, if you want to help."

I march to the refrigerator and pull out the lettuce, carrots, and celery.

I glance over at Zenith, wondering if she overheard our conversation. But she seems focused on solving her multiplication problems.

After we have prayed with Zenith and tucked her in for the night, Eric gets out his gym clothes. "I'm going next door," he says. "Brody and I are going to do squats tonight. Don't wait up."

I sit on the edge of our king-sized bed and watch Eric strip out of his shirt. If Zenith was taking biology, she would be able to name all the muscles just by examining her father's back.

I reach over and touch Eric below the waist. "I thought maybe you'd like to stay in tonight and have some fun with me."

He removes my hand and slips into a pair of running shorts. "Not now. I've had a long day. Between carpooling, housework, and the assortment of errands you leave me to do, I'm not in the mood for anything except pumping iron."

I lie down on the bed and stare at the ceiling. Is this how Eric felt when he used to come home and I would slip out for a few hours to attend a book club meeting and come home tipsy and giddy from wine and girl talk only to find him snoring loudly in bed with his back to me? Was he just as horny and lonely as I am right now? Does he just want to escape into a world of clanging metal and guy talk, just like I wanted to escape into a world of fictional characters and girl talk?

Eric slips on his weight-lifting gloves and bends to kiss my lips.

I wrap my arms around his neck and pull him close. He gently removes my arms and backs away.

"Don't look at me like that," he says. "I'm not a monster. Yeah, I snapped at you today. I'm sorry about that. But I'm not some horrible guy. I just need to get out."

Oh, my. If only I had been more understanding, then maybe I would be entitled to ask him to stay home tonight. But I had nagged him into allowing me to attend the book club. "It's just one night," I reasoned with him. "You won't even miss me." But between the other things I had volunteered to do, I was hardly home when he was home, and that was fine by me. Now it's not fine. I want to spend time with my husband, not read a book alone.

Maybe it's not too late. "I'm sorry I wasn't the perfect housewife. I should have been more understanding while you were working full-time."

"Don't worry about it." He bends to lace his shoes. "I've got a surprise for you this weekend. Something I hope you'll like."

"Really?" I sit up. "A surprise?"

"Don't go snooping around the house while I'm gone," he says, "because you won't find anything. It's not that type of surprise."

Hmm. I wonder what it could be.

Eric stands up. "Night."

"Have fun."

His footsteps echo down the hall. The front door clicks shut.

I lie back down and close my eyes. A surprise. For me. Hmm. What could it be? Tickets to the ballet? I've been dying to see Giselle. But we don't have any disposable income. Hmm. Maybe he won tickets to the Heart concert that they've been giving away on the radio. Oh, the possibilities.

Chapter 6

Fat Friday begins promptly at 8:30 a.m. when the courier delivers a banquet-sized box of donuts. I make an announcement on the loud speaker, "Breakfast is served," and the employees file into the break room like a herd of cattle for their fill of coffee and donuts before the 9:00 a.m. company-wide meeting in the upstairs conference room.

I never attend the meetings. I sit at my station, greeting clients, and answering phones. Only today, Frank swaggers into the lobby and stops by my desk rat-tat-tapping on the counter the drum solo from "Working Man."

"How's it going, babe?" he asks.

I smile. "Great. It's payday. The weekend is just hours away. And my husband has a surprise for me."

"Ah, yes, the blessed trinity—money, time, and romance." He winks. "I have a meeting today at 11 o'clock, and I'm wondering if you can do some prep work for me." He sets a stack of papers on my desk. "These are the minutes from all the board meetings of World Bank for the last five years. I need you to go through them and highlight anything of importance."

My shoulders tense. "How do I know what's important?"

"Imagine you're buying an art gallery, okay? You want to know which artists have shown their work over the years and what type of sales they've generated, as well as the general costs of running the business. And any anomalies. Like an insurance claim for $25,000 for the fire damage caused by an installation. Or the $10,000 shortage from a deeply discounted sale by an associate who did not know how to work the books. Those kinds of things, okay?"

I flip through the ream of paper and wonder how long it will take me to decipher everything.

"It's research," Frank explains. "It will aid in solidifying my negotiations, in case World Bank's Board of Directors decide to counter our offer."

Jeez. I was hoping for a quiet morning. Now, I've more work than I've had all week. "It's a lot to go through in two hours."

"You can do it." Frank slaps the counter and whistles, "Tonight, Tonight, Tonight," as he walks down the aisle toward the break room.

Boring, boring, boring. These minutes have nothing exciting in them. I don't know what Frank expects me to highlight. The increase in the monthly service cost for shredding? Or how about the $100,000 spent on office supplies?

A voice from Accounting drifts over the cubicles. "I don't believe she found that error. I swear the President gave her credit for the work because she gave him a blow job."

"Or a titty-fuck."

"That's right. Who wouldn't want to fuck those titties? They're the only thing holding up her bobble-headed brain."

A burst of giggles erupts from the cubicles next to me.

I flush with embarrassment and humiliation. How dare they accuse me of doing something unethical just because they don't believe I can do anything other than answer phones and smile pretty for incoming traffic?

Ignore them, I tell myself. But their tittering and joking continue to bandy back and forth until I'm frothing and foaming with anger.

I pick up the phone and dial Frank's office.

"What's up, babe?"

"I have a problem that I need to talk to you about. Immediately."

"Come on over."

I go into Jim's office and ask him to cover the phones. "I'll only be a couple of minutes," I tell him.

Jim glances up from his computer monitor and stares at my breasts. I'm wearing a purple Vine Valley Bank polo shirt that does not reveal anything. Part of me wishes I could just cut off my breasts and donate them to charity. But then, I'd be getting stares for not having a womanly figure and I'd be back to being the butt of jokes.

Sheesh. I can't seem to win, can I?

"If you don't want to watch the phones, I'll put them on night service," I tell him.

Jim shakes his head and stands up. "No, no, you go ahead. I'll watch them."

I stride down the aisle toward the President's suite. The women in Accounting hush as I walk by, only to erupt into a fit of giggles after I've turned the corner. The rest of the office pretends not to see me walking down the hall. I rap my knuckles on the President's door.

"Come in," he says.

I open the door and step into the office.

I've never been into the President's suite before. The walls are painted a dove gray and lined with bookcases. A huge window covers the entire wall behind Frank's desk. The view of the vineyards is absolutely breathtaking. For a moment, I forget why I am here. Look at all those luscious autumn colors! My fingers itch for a paint brush. What a terrific landscape it would make!

Frank clears his throat, grabbing my attention. He looks comfortably at home as he leans back in his leather executive chair with his feet propped on the desk and a stack of files in his lap. Bon Jovi sings, "Livin' on a Prayer," from his computer's speakers. "Close the door," he says.

My eyes widen in horror. "I can't do that," I say.

"Why not?" he asks.

My face flushes with anger. "People will think I'm having sex with you."

A serious expression hardens his face. Frank swings his feet off the desk, puts the stack of papers down, and strides across the room to shut the door. "Have a seat," he says.

I refuse to move. Doesn't he understand a thing I just said?

Frank shoves a chair toward me until it hits the back of my knees, forcing me to bend and sit like an obedient dog. "I'm going to take care of the problem once and for all," he says. "Don't say anything, okay?"

I gulp and nod.

Frank strides around his massive desk and turns down the music. "The first rule in business," he says, "is to give the public what they want." I open my mouth to protest, but he places a finger over his lips, reminding me to be quiet.

What is he going to do?

Frank sits down and turns on the intercom function on his phone. He leans forward like a general commanding an army, only the words coming out of his mouth sound like a pornographic movie. "Oh, god, that feels good," he moans.

I want to wither up and die. This is so embarrassing. How am I going to walk back to my desk without dying from humiliation?

Half-way through his X-rated show, Frank's sexy voice abruptly switches to a bark with bite. "Now that I have your attention, I want to announce that if anyone continues to harass Beverly Mael, I will personally escort you out of the building. Show's over. Get back to work!"

Frank turns off the intercom and gazes at me. A crooked smile plays at the corner of his lips. "How was that? Do you think I was as good as Meg Ryan in *When Harry Met Sally*?"

I want to strangle him. But I don't. I twist my sweaty hands in my lap, wishing I had never come in to see him.

"So, what did you want to talk to me about?" Frank leans back in his chair and twirls a pencil between his fingers.

I swallow. "You just addressed it."

He chuckles. "I can't believe you let that stuff bother you." He leans forward and gazes at me seriously. "Listen. There are two types of people in this world—players and spectators. Everyone out there gossiping about you is a spectator. Spectators do just what their name implies. They do not get things done. Players get things done. They are the movers and the shakers in this world, and they are the ones whose opinion I respect and whose advice I follow. So tell me, Bev, are you a spectator or a player?"

I gulp. Maybe he's right. The women in Accounting never seem to get any of their work done. They are always jabbering about other people, whether it is someone in the office or a celebrity they've read about in one of the rag magazines. People like Frank, on the other hand, always seem to be busy with big things, such as buying out World Bank. And, although I'm just a receptionist, Frank does not treat me like one. He treats me like I'm part of his team.

I sit up straight and meet his expectant gaze. "I'm a player," I say.

"That's what I thought." Frank grabs the stack of papers and props his legs on the desk. "Now, go out and play."

My legs wobble as I leave Frank's office. People glance up and gawk at me, but no one says a word. Even Jim stands up from my station and returns to his office without staring at my breasts. I sit down and wait a moment for the gossip to start. But all I hear is the rat-tat-tat of calculators and the chatter of fingers pressing keyboards. The phone rings and I answer it. I direct the call to Loan Servicing and hang up the line. The women in Accounting continue to work silently in their cubicles. Jim quietly stares at his computer monitor reading his e-mail. A new feeling of respect swells within me. I shove my sketchbook aside and grab the minutes Frank left me. I pick up a highlighter and start to read.

Chapter 7

That evening, I stand in front of our tiny closet and ask Eric how I should dress for our date. Eric sits on our bed, typing on his laptop. "I don't care if you wear jeans and a T-shirt, or your black dress and heels," he says without glancing up. "I just want you to be comfortable."

Hmm. That doesn't leave me with a whole lot of guesses about where we might be going. T-shirt and jeans—concert. Black dress and heels—ballet. I rifle through my clothes, trying to decide what I should wear.

After a few minutes, I spin around and say, "Just give me a hint about where we are going."

"No hints." Eric continues to type on his laptop. "That just ruins the fun."

I glower at him as he sits with the laptop across his folded legs. Why is he always on a computer? Can't he take a break for a moment and help me pick out something appropriate to wear?

But he doesn't seem to notice my frustration.

I turn back toward the closet. Ugh. I hate this. I guess I could dress down and bring accessories. That's a strategy that might work. After debating between several outfits for ten minutes, I finally decide on a plain ruby red dress. I tuck my pearls in a side pocket in my purse, just in case we do make it to the ballet. Otherwise, I have a chunky necklace and bangle bracelets for a concert. And if we go some place else, I can throw on a scarf. My purse is more the size of a carry-all tote. I even have room for a change of shoes.

Zenith peeks her head into the bedroom and asks, "Are you ready yet?" I am dropping her off at Mindi's house for a sleepover while Eric prepares for my surprise.

I spray my wrists with Mariah Carey's Mine Again perfume, which was a gift from Vi when I went back to work. The chocolate raspberry scent lingers on my skin. Zenith grabs my hand and sniffs my wrist. "Mmm. Yummy," she says. "Can I ask Ms. Patel if we can go to Cold Stone for dessert?"

"No, you may not," I tell her.

She pouts.

Guilt slowly overcomes me. Since I have been working, there have been no Mommy and Me play dates. The more upset Zenith becomes, the more I try to calm her down, even if it means buying her love—something I used to criticize other moms for doing. I search for my wallet and pull out a twenty dollar bill I've been saving for gas so I do not have to bike to work during rainy weather. I don't tell Zenith I am making a sacrifice. "Here. Give this to Ms. Patel, and tell her you would like to treat her and Mindi to dessert at Cold Stone."

Zenith jumps up and down and wraps her arms around me. "You're the best, Mommy."

Eric looks up from his laptop with a hurt expression on his face. "What about me? Am I chopped liver?"

Zenith climbs on the bed and kisses his cheek. "Oh, Daddy, don't be silly. I love you more."

"That's more like it." He rubs his stubble against her neck and she squeals with delight.

At a quarter after six, Zenith and I slip into our ancient Ford Escort and drive east. Vi lives in a townhouse on the hill overlooking Vine Valley. She used to own a mansion on the hill, but when she divorced Bob, they had to sell it. Downsizing for her is luxury for me. The sun is setting in the west by the time we arrive. The view is breathtaking. You can see the entire valley to the Pacific Ocean from the front steps of her townhouse.

"There you are," Vi says, opening the door.

Zenith rushes inside and hugs Mindi. The two girls bound up the stairs, leaving Vi and me alone.

"Come in," Vi says.

"I only have a moment," I tell her. "Eric is planning a surprise for me. I can hardly wait."

Vi smiles and escorts me into the living room. I sit down on the loveseat facing the gas fireplace that hides the big screen TV. Vi curls up on the recliner.

"How have you been?" she asks.

I shrug. "Busy at the bank. The President keeps giving me more and more work. But I don't mind, because it makes time go by faster." I don't want to tell her about the rumors being spread about me, or the way Frank handled the gossip. "What's new with you?"

Vi wraps her arms around her knee and pulls it to her chest. "I've met someone."

"Really?"

She nods. "He's a doctor. And he lives in Anaheim. So it's a long distance relationship. But that's okay. We met on MyMate.com."

"Do your parents know?"

Since her divorce, Vi's parents have been trying to get her to agree to a traditional arranged marriage with a family friend in India.

"Not yet. It's not serious. We mostly chat online or text between clients. Next weekend, he's coming up here for our first visit. I'm counting on you to take Mindi overnight."

"Of course. That's what friends are for."

I sit back against the soft leather and imagine Vi dating a doctor. Why couldn't I have fallen in love with a wealthy doctor? Or a dentist? Or a stockbroker? Or an even an insurance salesman, like Vi's ex-husband, Bob, who makes $250,000 a year? Why did I fall for a guy who likes to play with computers and break all the rules? Seriously, what was I thinking?

"That reminds me," I say. "Do you know of any father's groups Eric could join? He's been hanging out with the boy next door, and he's starting to show signs of teenage rebellion."

Vi snickers. "Eric? A teenager? Bev, he's always been that way. You were just too in love to notice."

Was I? No, that can't be right. When I met Eric, he was a mature, responsible young man with a dream of working for the National Security Agency. Sure, he liked to play practical jokes on his roommate and stay up late playing video games, but he also worked his way through college and skipped lunch for six months to save up enough money to buy me an engagement ring. By the time Vi met him, Eric was working full-time in the IT department. Sure, it wasn't his dream job, but at least he wasn't stuck flipping burgers at McDonald's. In all the years I've known him, Eric's never had a problem managing his emotions, until I started working and he started caring for Zenith and the house. I remember the early days of motherhood, when a lack of sleep and a lack of adult interaction sent me over the edge into post-partum depression. Maybe Eric is experiencing something similar to it: a post-lay-off-rage-against-the-world syndrome.

"I think he needs to be with other stay-at-home dads, just like we were in a mother's group back when our kids were little."

She taps her lower lip with her finger as she thinks. "I'll have to check with the others at the office. I'm sure I can find one if they exist."

"They should. More and more dads are staying home. And they need solidarity. They face discrimination and prejudice. Sometimes even from the people in their lives."

"Gosh, Bev, I didn't know this was such a hot button."

My eyes smart. I'm thinking about the women in Accounting who think I am only a pretty face. "I know how it feels to be misjudged, and I don't want Eric to feel that way. I really appreciate him stepping up to the task of being Mr. Mom while I work. The transition hasn't been easy for either one of us, and I'm really glad he's so good at taking care of things. He even cooks better than I do."

Vi reaches over and touches my hand. "I'll see what I can find."

I glance at my watch. It's almost seven. "I have to go," I say.

"Give Eric my love," Vi says, waving to me from the front door.

"I will." I hop into the Escort and drive down the hill.

I arrive home in a few minutes. Eric waits for me in the living room with a huge smile on his face. "I'm driving," he says, reaching for my keys.

I slip into the passenger side of the Escort. Eric reaches over and places a scarf over my eyes. "It's part of the surprise," he explains. "I don't want you to know where we're going until we get there."

At first, I resist, but then I finally decide to just go with it.

I hear the trunk pop open and Eric moving around the outside of the vehicle before sitting down beside me and closing the door. "Ready?" he asks.

I nod. My hands tingle with anticipation. We're going on an adventure.

Eric drives slowly and methodically. Silence fills the space between us. We haven't been alone on a date in months. It feels odd to be sitting beside him, blindfolded, without the radio blasting and Zenith singing a Top 40 song at the top of her lungs. I twist my hands in my lap. Why won't he tell me where we're going? Or at least say something, so I know he's still here beside me and hasn't turned into a psycho stranger who plans to maim me in the hills and bury me in a ravine. Maybe I should say something. But how do you make conversation while blindfolded? You can't play I Spy, because you can't see. And talking about the weather seems pointless. Still, it would be better than this painful quiet.

"How long have you been planning this surprise?" I ask.

A moment of silence stretches between us. "Three years," he says.

Three years? Did I hear him correctly? "How can you have been planning a surprise date for three years?"

"Well, good dates are hard to come by. And good surprises are even harder," he says. "Are you excited?"

I shrug. "It's hard to be completely comfortable, not knowing where we're going or what we're going to do once we get there."

Eric parks and turns off the engine. "Well, you don't have to wait any longer. We're here."

"Can I take off the blindfold?"

"Not yet." Eric gets out of the car and opens the trunk. He returns a bit later and says, "Open your mouth."

Okay. This is not what I expected. It sounds a bit too kinky for me. Where's the crowd of people milling about waiting to see Heart? Where's the tinkle of expensive diamond bracelets on women going to see the ballet? And why does Eric want me to open my mouth?

Eric places something smooth and cool against my pursed lips and wedges it into my mouth. I take a tentative bite. It's a grape. He's feeding me grapes.

Is this a joke?

Eric feeds me strawberries and kiwi and bananas while I'm blindfolded in the car. He asks me to name each fruit he places in my mouth. I finally realize we are not going to a concert or the ballet. We are going to stay parked here, wherever here is, and eat fruit until Eric runs out of food.

"Isn't this romantic?" Eric asks.

"It's one sided," I tell him. "I'm the one who can't see anything. You, on the other hand, get to see everything."

Eric removes the blindfold. "Is that better?"

I blink a few times until my eyes focus. Eric gazes at me longingly. He brushes his fingertips against the nape of my neck and draws me close for a long, sweet, slow, and deep kiss.

When he releases me, I tentatively glance around. My hopes sink. We are parked at the far end of the Home Depot parking lot overlooking the valley. A streak of light burns against the horizon, and a blanket of stars start to pinprick the deep blue sky. We're the only ones here. In the backseat, fruits and cheese, and a bottle of champagne we've been saving peek out from a picnic basket next to Eric's laptop bag. Eric cups the back of my neck. His lips feel soft and warm against my mouth. The initial disappointment melts away with each kiss. My whole body tingles with delight. I feel like a naughty teenager making out in her parents' car. I hope the cops don't come by and ask us to leave.

"Surprised?" Eric asks.

I nod.

He opens the bottle of champagne and pours two glasses. "A toast to our new life," he says.

We sit in the car, drinking champagne and eating cheese on crackers. The full moon rises above the twinkling city lights. Eric checks his watch. "I have one more surprise," he says. "Keep watching the lights."

Okay. I wonder what the last surprise is. I face forward in the seat and stare at the city lights. Eric glances at his watch. "Thirty seconds."

I glance at him. What is he doing?

"Keep looking at the lights," he says.

I turn back to the window. The lights glow like tiny fireflies.

"Ten, nine," he counts down.

When he reaches zero, the entire city goes black. The only light remaining is the moon, which seems to be laughing in the sky. I swivel in my seat. "What happened?"

"Look." He points toward the dark city. Like a kid flicking on a light switch, the entire city bursts into light.

Slowly, the pieces come together like a puzzle. How Eric is always working on the computer whenever he has a free moment. How he has been planning this surprise date for three years. How he not only knew the exact moment of the blackout, but the exact moment the lights would turn back on. Suddenly, the euphoria of the romantic evening evaporates. My whole body numbs with fear. "*You* did that."

He chuckles. "It's pretty amazing, isn't it?"

I bat his arm. "What will PG&E say?"

"They won't know. I've covered my footprints." He laughs until tears glisten in his eyes. "The script makes it look like an internal system error."

"Is this what you've been working on all these years?"

He nods. "I've got a few other things planned, but not for tonight."

"I don't believe you," I say, sinking back into my seat. The fear dissolves into anger. I clench my fists, ready to punch the dashboard. "You better not get caught," I tell him. "PG&E won't be as kind as the company you worked for was. These guys will press charges. You'll be locked up for life."

"Don't worry," Eric says. "I know what I'm doing."

I glance over at him and wonder if he truly understands the magnitude of his actions. This is not just one big practical joke. This is serious. He's messing with someone else's toys and he might get caught. Then what will Zenith and I do? Visit him at prison? Write him love letters and send him photographs? Or file for divorce and start dating on MyMate.com?

I sigh. Maybe Vi's right. Eric has been, and always will be, a perpetual teenager and I've just been too blinded by love to see it.

Chapter 8

As soon as we get home, Eric logs onto the computer and checks the local news. Already, there is a blurb about the incident. "Power Outage Seizes City" reads the headline. I glance over his shoulder and read the article. "PG&E technicians are investigating the black-out" it begins. My palms start to sweat. What if they find out it was my husband? What will happen to us?

Eric bursts into laughter. "Listen to this. 'Technicians suspect an internal system error may have caused the outage.'"

A ripple of relief snakes through me. Maybe everything will be all right. Maybe no one will know it was Eric. But then I remember Eric saying he has a few other things planned. My body tenses with anger. What other things?

"This is the best news I've read in years," Eric says.

I cross my arms over my chest. "You're just as bad as a serial killer reading the papers to see if anyone mentions his handiwork."

"Yeah, baby, that's me." He flashes a cheesy grin.

I slap his arm. "This isn't funny. You're dealing with things you have no right to mess with."

Eric pulls me into his lap. I struggle to get away, but he's too strong. "Listen," he says, "it's not as bad as you make it out to be." The smile vanishes from his face. He gazes at me solemnly. "I didn't hurt anyone."

Not this time, I think, although I do not say anything.

Eric tries to break my serious mood by tickling me, but I resist. "What happened to your sense of humor?" he asks. "Did corporate America swallow it?"

What happened to my husband? I want to ask. Did staying home turn him into a cyber criminal?

"I'm tired," I say. "I think I'll go to bed."

Eric tries to kiss me, but I turn my head away. "You're still mad at me," he says.

"Wouldn't you be?" I ask.

"No," he says, matter-of-factly. "I would be proud you accomplished what you set out to do."

"Why should I be proud of you breaking the law?"

Eric shakes his head. "You don't understand, do you? This is my life. This is what I do."

"Of course, I understand. I know this is who you are. I've never once complained about how much time you spend in front of those machines. Never. What I don't understand, and what I cannot accept, is how selfish you can be. You didn't even think through your actions. What if you get caught? What will happen then? Do you have a backup plan for that?"

Eric takes a deep breath and exhales sharply. "Why don't you believe in me and my talent? I always encourage you to continue painting, even when your parents ridicule you for not earning any money from it. I understand it is part of your life. Don't you understand that breaking things and fixing things are part of mine?"

"But this is illegal," I say.

Eric shakes his head. "I don't want to spend the rest of my life being a has-been masquerading as a stay-at-home-dad. I want to be a cyber star."

A cyber star? Like a rock star, or a movie star? How juvenile is that? "Keep dreaming," I say.

"I'm not a dreamer," Eric says. "I'm a doer. See what I've done." He points to the monitor. "People notice my work. It's important."

"It's so important, you will risk getting caught by the authorities," I say. "You will let me worry about how I am going to support us, while you rot away in prison."

"I'm not going anywhere," Eric says. "Stop being so melodramatic."

I stomp down the hall and slam the bedroom door. Our wedding photo rattles on the wall. I open my jewelry box and dig out the rosary I prayed every night when I was trying to find a job. I make the Sign of the Cross and kneel down beside the bed and pray for God to get through to Eric, because I certainly cannot.

The next morning, I wake in a panic. Eric snores beside me, oblivious to the thud-thud-thudding in my chest. I get up and check the lights in the house. Everything seems to be working just fine. I think about going to the corner store to pick up a newspaper, but then reconsider it. Why ruin my weekend with more bad news?

I open a diet soda and sink into the sofa. My gaze focuses on the computer in the corner of the room. What should I do? If I discontinue our Internet service, Eric might connect to Brody's wireless network and continue to surf while I'm at work. If I confiscate his laptop, he'll still have the computer in the house. If I get rid of both the laptop and the home computer, he might find someone willing to loan them theirs. I tuck my legs under my hips and sip my diet soda. Hmm. I'm running out of options.

By the time Eric pads into the living room rubbing his bald head and yawning, I've already decided to consult with the IT department at work. Surely, someone at the bank knows all about computer security and can help me brainstorm a solution.

Eric turns on the computer and brings up the headlines. "Look at this," he says, pointing to a photograph of the darkened city. His smile fades when he glances over at me. "You're still angry."

I stand up and move into the kitchen to make breakfast.

Eric follows me. "I don't know what your problem is. Some companies hire guys like me to help them secure their networks."

"Then find one to hire you," I snap.

"Is this about me being unemployed?" he asks. "You know I've tried getting a job."

I remove eggs from the refrigerator and crack a few open and beat them furiously before pouring them into the heated skillet.

Eric stares at the eggs. "I thought you said you didn't mind going back to work."

"I lied." I wipe my hands and slap the towel against the counter. "It's not like we had a lot of options. We went through our savings and my parents don't have money to spare. The inheritance your parents left when they died ran out. What else was I going to do? Suggest we file for bankruptcy?"

"So that's what this is all about. You're bitter about working and you're taking it out on me."

"I am not bitter about working. Things are actually going very well. The President gave me some figures that Accounting couldn't sort out, and treated me to lunch when I solved the problem." I turn down the heat on the stove and remove plates from the cupboard. "I'm angry with you for breaking into PG&E."

Eric stares at me while I place bread in the toaster. "He likes you."

"What?"

"The President wants you."

I shove the loaf of bread into the refrigerator and slam the door. "He respects me and the work I do." I don't want to go into the entire *When Harry Met Sally* performance Frank gave for the benefit of the bank, but I don't want Eric to think Frank is just another admirer of my breasts. "Besides, we're both married."

"That doesn't matter," Eric says. "Marriage doesn't stop people from cheating."

"Are you accusing me of cheating?"

Eric places silverware on the table. "I think you should stay away from the guy. He sounds like he's preying on you."

"Frank isn't like that," I say.

"Does he take anyone else out to lunch?"

Does he? Hmm. He's taken members of the Board of Directors out for lunch and he's dined with a few potential new clients, but I can't recall the last time he treated an employee to lunch.

Eric takes my silence as proof of Frank's guilt. "I'm right. He thinks you're hot."

"Just because you think I'm hot, doesn't mean everyone else does."

"But you *are* hot."

Jeez. I'm not that attractive. My eyes are too small and my nose is too big. And I'm short. What good is being short?

"What time are we picking up Zenith?" I ask.

"You're changing the subject," Eric says.

"I'm done with the subject."

Eric places butter on the table and pours orange juice in glasses. "Eleven o'clock."

Good. That leaves us two hours. Surely, I can find a way to be civil to my husband for two measly hours.

I serve the eggs and toast and sit at the farthest spot from Eric. We glower at each other in a tense moment of silence, before Eric bows his head and makes the Sign of the Cross.

When we arrive at eleven o'clock to pick up our daughter, Vi greets us at the door with hugs. "Come in," she says, waving us inside. "I just made some fresh naan. Want some?"

"No, thanks," Eric says. "I'm cutting down on carbs."

Vi squeezes his bicep. "You're getting pretty buff."

He flashes a modest smile and shrugs. "I've got a long way to go to look the way I want to look."

"And how is that?" Vi asks.

"Like Branch Warren. He won the 2009 Mr. Olympia competition in Las Vegas."

"Are you going to compete?" Vi asks.

"Not this year," Eric says. What he fails to tell her is the cost involved in a body building competition. Eric would need a sponsor to pay for the training, supplements, and food. And if he can't get a job, what makes him think he could get a sponsor?

I wander into the kitchen and grab a piece of naan. It's soft and warm and feels so comforting. "Mmm. This is good," I say between bites.

"Thanks. It's my mom's recipe."

"How is your mother doing?" Eric asks. "Is she still nagging you to agree to an arranged marriage?"

"Of course, but I don't believe in arranged marriages."

Eric stands by the window and gazes at the view of the valley. "I think arranged marriages are best," Eric says. "It's like working for a company. You have a job to do and you do it and it doesn't matter whether or not you're happy. The job gets done."

Vi glances from Eric to me. Her eyebrows lift with unasked questions.

I go upstairs to get the girls.

Zenith and Mindi sit cross-legged on the pearly white carpet of Mindi's pastel pink bedroom playing with Polly Pocket dolls. I stand in the doorway just admiring them for a moment. Their hair is shiny in the late morning sun, and innocent smiles grace their faces.

Zenith takes a doll and sits her on a chair in front of a desk. "I'm going to hack into Vine Valley Bank and transfer money into my account," she says.

"You can't do that," Mindi says. "My network is too secure."

"Says who?"

"Says me."

I freeze. Is this what my husband has been teaching them since I've gone back to work? Hacking and network security. Whatever happened to reading, writing, and arithmetic?

Zenith glances up from playing. "Hi, Mommy!" she beams.

Mindi smiles. "Hello, Mrs. Mael. How are you?"

"F—f—fine," I stutter. But I'm not fine. I'm anything but fine.

Without a word, Mindi starts gathering the dolls and putting them into a carrying case. Zenith follows her lead.

"I'll be downstairs," I tell them.

In the kitchen, Vi and Eric sit at the small circular table drinking chai and talking about the brief power outage last night.

"The girls and I were watching *Avatar*," Vi says. "The whole house went dark and when we gazed outside, we could not see anything. It looked like a black ocean."

"Yeah, it was amazing, wasn't it?" He sips his chai and eyes me.

My whole body tenses. I want to pull Vi into the other room and tell her the truth, but I can't. I can't even tell her how our children have been influenced by my husband in how they view the world when they play.

I go into the living room like a coward and sit on the leather sofa and wait. The long staircase and high ceilings make the townhouse seem bigger than it is. I lean back and imagine living in a place with immaculate white walls and plush white carpeting with the faint scent of vanilla lingering in the air. Part of me knows my life would not be any easier or simpler with a bigger, better house, but the other part of me cannot stop daydreaming.

A few minutes later, the girls bound down the stairs. Zenith sets her overnight bag at the foot of the stairs and gives her friend a long hug goodbye.

"All ready?" Vi asks.

Eric picks up the overnight bag like it is a piece of tissue. With his other arm, he grabs Zenith by the waist and swings her around until she giggles. We look like a happy family as we head out to the Escort beneath a mild October sky, but I feel like I've been pasted into the picture and the edges are coming loose and starting to peel away.

Chapter 9

On Monday, Emilio returns to work with his wavy black hair slicked back from his forehead and his bronze skin even tanner than before. "I just got back from Mexico last night." He selects a lollipop from the glass jar on the counter and tosses the wrapper on my desk. "You should have seen the city when we flew in. Pitch black. The pilot thought we were going to have to circle around till the power came back on. Luckily, it didn't take long."

Damn, Eric. I can't escape from his childish prank. Not even here in the sanctity of work.

As soon as Emilio leaves, Frank strolls into the bank whistling a song I've heard, but can't place. "How was your weekend, babe?" he asks.

I narrow my eyes in disgust. "Not great. How about you?"

He sets a newspaper on the counter and his briefcase on the floor and plucks the lollipop wrapper from my desk and tosses it in the trash bin underneath my desk. "It must have been bad for you to eat candy for breakfast."

I laugh. "That wasn't me."

He leans against my desk and crosses his arms over his chest and thinks. "I have a few assignments this week for you. Information gathering, mostly. Emilio will take care of the routine stuff, but I want you to focus on World. I've been thinking about them all weekend, trying to figure out what's really going on, and I think I'm going to need a woman's touch. Kind of like Erin Brockovich. Are you up for the challenge?"

I nod. "Unless it involves anything illegal or immoral."

He lifts his eyebrows. "Why did you say that?"

Tears start to push their way to my eyes. Why do I feel like crying? It must be that time of month. I wish I wasn't so emotional. Maybe I should switch to decaf. "I just don't want to break into their network to see what's really going on."

He taps my desk with his fingers. "The type of information I'm looking for involves numbers and human interest. Can you interpret the statistics printed in a spreadsheet? Or read between the lines of a press release?"

Sounds like more boring investigative work that leads to nothing that makes sense to me. But Frank is asking me to do it. So it must have some relevance. I shrug. "I'll do my best."

He glances at my work space. "Where's your sketchbook?"

Between the extra responsibilities at work and the tension at home, I have had no desire to pick up a pencil. "I didn't bring it."

"Why not?"

"I'm busy."

Frank touches my shoulder briefly. The pressure from his fingertips against my blouse startles me. I lift my head. He bends and whispers in my ear, "Bring it. It inspires you. And I need for you to be inspired."

In the afternoon, between phone calls, I study the spreadsheets Frank has given me from World Bank. The maturity report shows past due loans for the past year. Hmm. Quite a few of these loans have disappeared and no longer show up anywhere. When I asked Frank what that means, he said either the Loan Officer was able to negotiate a change in terms that the borrower was able to honor, or the loan was moved into non-accrual so it no longer shows up on any of the reports. "I'm in the process of finding out how many loans are not accounted for," he says. "It's not unusual for banks to redistribute their portfolio when they're in trouble. It shows stockholders that things are better than they are, which I think is the case with World."

Hmm. I wish I could move my assets around so that my charge cards from Nieman Marcus, Victoria's Secret, and Macy's no longer showed up on any of our monthly statements. Then I could replenish my wardrobe without it affecting our daily budget.

When I get back from my fifteen minute break, Damon, the lanky, long-haired guy from the IT department, hovers over my computer. "What's wrong?" he asks, tapping at the keyboard. "You seem to have all of your security updates."

I flush. "Umm. Actually it was more of a general question."

"Oh, a GQ. Go head. Ask." He stops typing and faces me.

I swallow, unsure of how to begin. "Well, I was wondering what security measures we have installed to prevent someone from hacking into our customers' accounts and transferring money."

A slight smile tugs at the corners of his thin lips. Is he mocking me?

"Hackers don't try to break into our network directly," he explains. "They usually phish out information from individuals through their e-mail accounts by sending bogus messages asking individuals to log into their accounts from a false link so they can capture the passwords by recording the keystrokes."

That doesn't sound like something Eric is working on. Maybe this guy doesn't know as much as Eric does.

"Well, what about a terrorist attack?"

He snickers. "Terrorists don't attack banks through their computer network. They bomb buildings."

This isn't getting me very far, is it? I glance down at the maturity report and receive a flash of inspiration. "What if another bank wanted to know how many bad loans we have? Couldn't they hack into our system and find out?"

Damon frowns. "Why would another bank want to risk Federal prosecution?"

I shrug. "You never know. In this economic climate, things happen, right? I mean, stockholders want to know what's really going on and we need to be able to keep our secrets, right?"

Damon shakes his head. "Really, what does this have to do with answering the phones?"

I lift the stack of spreadsheets on my desk and show him. "I'm doing some research for Frank and he thinks World Bank is hiding something from the public. Couldn't someone hack into their computer system and find out the truth?"

Damon takes the spreadsheets from my hands and shakes his head. "Really, Bev, you shouldn't worry yourself over things like this. We have our ways to keep things confidential."

"But knowledge is power," I say, "so the more informed I am, the better I am able to support your efforts to protect the bank."

He hands me the spreadsheets and shakes his head. "Really, Bev, I think you should just go back to answering the phones. The questions you're asking are way above what you need to know to do your job."

I sigh. He's not going to tell me anything.

For a long moment, I consider telling Damon the truth about my sudden interest in computers. But I know compromising my husband's secret will only jeopardize the family. The last thing I need is the police at my front door seizing the computer and interrogating Zenith about her daddy.

Then another thought occurs to me. Damon doesn't take me seriously. He thinks I am a joke. A pretty girl typing pretty memos and worrying about maturity reports, because she watches too many night time dramas on TV.

I thank Damon for his time. After he leaves, I pick up the phone and call Vi on her office line. She is probably with a client, since she does not answer. I leave a message. "Call me," I say. "I'm at the bank. You have the number. No e-mails or texts, please. I want to talk."

At a quarter to four, Vi calls. "I'm sorry it's taken so long to return your call," she says, "but I've been trying to find a father's group for Eric."

I smile falsely at one of the women from Accounting leaving early for the day. As soon as the glass door closes behind her, I say, "I don't know if that will help as much as I'd like it to. Our problems are bigger than that now."

"I imagine from that comment he made about arranged marriages yesterday. Do you want to go to lunch tomorrow and talk about it?"

I tap at my keyboard. "I have an eleven-thirty tomorrow with Frank to discuss World. But I can meet you at the Tea Room at one."

"That's great," Vi says. Lowering her voice, she adds, "Will you be all right tonight?"

I shrug. "Why shouldn't I be?" Between my husband trying to take over the world one computer at a time and my daughter who wants to be just like him, I think I'll spend a wonderful evening sitting in front of the TV, sipping diet soda, and pretending everything is just fine.

Chapter 10

When I arrive home, the living room is empty. The computer is turned off. I slip off my heels and pad down the hall. "Eric! Zenith!" Silence echoes back at me. I knock on the bathroom door before opening it. No one is there. I glance into Zenith's bedroom. Nothing. I step into my bedroom and shut the door and change into a soft T-shirt and comfy jeans. Outside, I hear voices. I glance out the window. Eric kicks a soccer ball to Zenith. She swings her leg and misses. "C'mon, focus," Eric yells. "Pretend I'm the goalie."

I spy Eric's laptop in the messenger bag at the foot of our bed. My heart beat races. Maybe I'll just check to see what he's been working on. It can't hurt, can it? Slowly, I drag the laptop bag across the floor and into the bathroom and shut and lock the door. On the cool tiles, I sit and wait for the laptop to start.

"That's it!" Eric shouts.

Zenith mutters something and Eric says, "Let's switch sides. You're the goalie now."

My palms sweat. I wipe my hands on my jeans and click on the icon beside Eric's name. A white box pops up asking for the password. Hmm. What could it be? I try Eric's password to the computer in the living room, 1buffd@d, but nothing happens.

Think, think, think.

"That's it," Eric shouts. "Don't let me make a goal!"

I try various other passwords I think Eric might use: buffd@d2, gymr@t, h@rdbody3, and fitg33k4, but nothing works.

The backdoor to the kitchen opens. I shut off the laptop, shove it back into the messenger bag, unlock the bathroom door, and place the bag at the foot of the bed where I found it. I hurry back into the bathroom, close the door, flush the toilet and run the water. My heart flutters in my chest like a bird trying to escape. The bedroom door opens and Eric says, "I didn't hear you come in. Dinner's almost ready."

"Great." I dry my hands on a towel and glimpse my flushed cheeks in the mirror.

Eric steps into the bathroom, pulls me close, and nuzzles my neck with the stubble on his chin. I giggle. He smells of freshly mown lawn and musky sweat. "I'm hungry," he says. He tugs me closer and nibbles on my earlobe. "Can we skip dinner and head straight to dessert?"

"Umm. I'd love to, but—"

"Dad! The timer is buzzing."

Eric slowly releases me. "Saved by the bell." He winks. "Consider that an appetizer."

When he is gone, I sink down on the edge of the mattress and take a few deep breaths. The laptop stares up at me like a reprimanding eye. I turn away, hoping Eric won't notice I've been snooping.

The next day, I hurry down the steps of the parking garage to meet Vi at the Tea Room for lunch. The sky is overcast and gray. I tug the sweater tightly over my breasts and listen to my heels clip-clop against the pavement. People mill around the corner, waiting for the streetlight to change ever since an overanxious meter maid started passing out tickets for jaywalking three weeks ago.

After crossing the street, I push open the heavy door to the Tea Room with its Victorian décor. The light scent of warm tea and fresh pastries welcomes me. Vi waves to me from across the room. I stride across the hardwood floors and Vi stands up to embrace me. "You sounded terrible yesterday," she says. "What's wrong?"

I sit down at the mahogany table and gaze out the window at the beauty salon across the street. Should I tell her about spying on Eric? Or should I just casually mention my paranoia between ordering lunch and chit-chatting about what the girls are going to be for Halloween?

When I don't answer, Vi takes out a piece of paper and slips it across the table. A list of father's groups in Vine Valley complete with names, phone numbers, websites, and e-mail addresses are written in Vi's loopy script. "I hope this helps," she says.

"Thanks." I fold the paper and tuck it carefully into a zippered pocket of my purse. "I've been worried about Eric spending so much time on the computer and with the kids."

Vi nods and pours me a cup of oolong tea from the pot she ordered. "I understand your concern, but I wouldn't worry about Eric. He volunteers at the school and spends time with you. It's not like he's holed up in a closet playing video games all day."

A waitress dressed in a frilly apron and a pencil tucked behind her ear asks if she can take our order.

Vi orders a curry cucumber sandwich and I order roast beef on a croissant. After the waitress leaves, I twist the napkin in my lap and sigh.

"Don't worry," Vi says. "Eric is fine. It's you I'm worried about."

"Me?"

She removes a newspaper from her briefcase and unfolds it to a story about World Bank. "I think your boss is using you to get a little something extra on the side," she says.

I frown at the headline, "World Bank Reports Strong Finish to Third Quarter." I skim the article, looking for clues, but find nothing except the regular media hype.

Vi studies me. "I think your boss made up that story about buying them out just to make you feel important, so you'll want to offer him your body as gratitude for his kindness."

"Why would he do that?" My eyes widen with disbelief. "I met the President of World Bank. I've seen their numbers. They're hiding their liabilities through creative accounting, and Frank wants me to ferret out the truth. He trusts me."

Vi shakes her head in sympathy and reaches out to touch me, but I pull away.

"Just because I didn't finish college doesn't mean I'm stupid." When Eric and I started dating, I attended a few classes at the junior college, but could not get motivated enough to finish. By the time I was pregnant with Zenith, I had given up on school.

Vi leans forward and whispers, "I never said you were stupid."

"Then why do you say things to make me think that you do?" I take a breath and try to steady my voice. "Frank doesn't make me feel stupid. He gives me important work to do. He respects me."

"Ah, honey, that's part of his plan to seduce you."

My eyes widen in horror.

Vi gazes at me with a sorrowful expression. "I'm just trying to protect you. I don't want to see your marriage to Eric jeopardized because of this job. I mean, you heard him this weekend, talking about the value of arranged marriages."

I want to laugh, but I don't. Vi doesn't know what inspired that comment. No one does. And no one will. Unless I decide to tell, which I won't.

The waitress brings our sandwiches. We eat in silence. Every now and then, I glance out the window at the passing traffic and the people strolling along the sidewalk on their way to meetings or restaurants or shopping. Vi does not mention anything else. Her focus seems entirely on my boss' supposed ulterior motives. If I was eating lunch with Frank, he would talk about the bank, about my art, about what's important and what's not. He would not bring the conversation to my breasts, or my lack of education. But Vi does not understand that. And, for the first time in our friendship, I feel lonely, disrespected, and misunderstood.

By the time the waitress brings our check, I have already placed my debit card on the table. Vi tries to give it back to me, insisting this is a business expense. That's when I realize she thinks I need help. Psychological help. From her.

Even though I can't really afford it, I shove the bill and my debit card into the pocket of the waitress' apron. Vi frowns her disapproval, but I don't care anymore what Vi thinks, because Vi doesn't believe I can think.

When I return to the office, dejected and in need of a severe pick-me-up, I find Emilio sitting at my desk. He taps the blunt end of a pencil against the keyboard and frowns. "Traitor," he spits.

"What?" I step back, afraid of his venom.

Emilio stands up and shakes the pencil at me. "You don't have the decency to wait till I get a new job, do you? You try to steal the one I have right under my nose, eh?"

"What are you talking about?"

"You can't play dumb with me. I know better. You've been sneaking around behind my back and working directly for Frankie when Jim's your boss. Am I right, or am I right?" He leans against the counter and crosses his arms and legs.

This is not what I need. Not a belligerent, disgruntled, dissatisfied male Executive Assistant accusing me of taking his job from him. "Listen. You were on vacation and Frank asked me to go with him to his meeting to take notes. That's it."

Emilio picks up a stack of spreadsheets. "So, what's this? Scratch paper? For you to draw on like a kindergartner between calls?" He scatters the sheets of paper over the floor.

What a mess. I bend down to gather the documents, but Emilio squats beside me and hisses, "You better be glad I got that offer from World for twice as much as this jerk pays me."

My mouth twitches. So that's where Frank got his insider news.

"I'll be gone in two weeks, but if I was staying, you can bet I'd make your life hell." Emilio stares at my breasts and nods. "You think you're more than a pretty face?"

I stand up and slam the papers against the desk. The vase of orchids rattles. "I know I am. And it's too bad you won't be here to see me prove it."

Chapter 11

At six o'clock, completely wiped out and ready for a good, hot meal, an even hotter bath, and a long night doing absolutely nothing, I arrive home to find Eric on the computer and the phone.

"Yes, that's no problem," he says, while typing. "I'm sure I can handle it. You need your rest."

Who is he talking to? And why is he Googling, "preeclampsia"?

"I'll send you a link. What's your e-mail address? Okay. Remember, you can buy that body pillow online. I'll send a link to that, too."

Zenith runs down the hall and slides to a stop next to me. She throws her arms around my waist and smiles up at me. "I got 100 percent on my spelling pre-test."

I stroke her hair. "That's wonderful, dear." Part of my attention keeps wandering over to Eric in the corner of the room.

"Mommy! Can we play Sorry after dinner?"

"Sure, honey." If we eat soon, play the game, and help Zenith to bed by eight, I can soak in the tub for an hour. "What are we having for dinner?"

"Whatever you're going to make," she says.

I lift my eyebrows. Eric has not started dinner. That's not like him. I glance down at Zenith. "Want to help me cook?"

"Sure, Mommy. What are we going to make?"

In the kitchen, I pull out a bag of pre-washed salad mix and a package of pre-cooked sausage, and leftover boiled potatoes. "You can toss the salad while I fry up sausage and potatoes, okay?"

A few moments later, Eric pads into the kitchen and rubs the stubble on his chin. "Sorry I haven't started dinner," he says. "I've been kind of busy."

"Who were you talking to?" I ask, trying to keep my voice even.

"Oh, that's Lori."

"She's Gina's mom," Zenith says.

Eric swivels around and narrows his eyes at Zenith, who seems to shrink a size smaller. "Daddy wasn't finished talking. You always need to wait till someone has stopped talking before you begin talking. Otherwise, you're interrupting and that's rude. If you do it again, you're going to be sent to your room for ten minutes, got it?"

Zenith nods and goes back to dumping the lettuce into a big plastic bowl.

Eric nudges me aside and heats the skillet. I move the butcher board to the other counter and start slicing sausage and potato wedges. A faint scent of garlic olive oil fills the air.

Eric turns the heat down low and waits for me to finish cutting. "Anyway, Lori's been ordered to bed rest till she delivers the twins she's carrying. She called to ask if I would be the interim room parent while she's out." Eric flashes a triumphant smile. "I told her I would do it."

I can't believe Eric is going to be a room parent. I could not get that coveted position when I volunteered in Zenith's second grade classroom. Heidi Malone got elected for that job, because she was the most experienced.

"How did you get elected?"

Eric casually shrugs. "I guess they like how I help out in the classroom."

Zenith raises her hand and jumps up and down, hoping we'll notice.

"Yes," Eric says. "You may talk."

Zenith's eyes glow with delight. "Daddy found this amazing site where you can build your own space shuttle and virtually test it."

"Oh, really?" I ask. That's it. The students did not appreciate the art docent lesson on the Impressionists I gave to them. They prefer to learn about space shuttles on the computer.

"And Daddy makes all the mommies laugh with his jokes. And when the other students tackle him on the playground, he doesn't fall over and get mad like Mr. Russell does. He just chases us. If he catches us, he tickles us."

I hand the sausages and potatoes to Eric. He slides them off the butcher board. They sizzle and pop in the skillet.

"Daddy's the most popular adult in the whole school."

Eric tries to hide the smile that is slowly spreading across his face, but the longer I stare at him, the harder it is for him to contain his glee.

"So how did the geekiest guy in college get voted the most popular guy in elementary school?" I ask.

He runs his hand over his bald dome. "Must be my hair."

I smack his shoulder playfully and shake my head. "Really, Mr. Mom, you never cease to amaze me."

Long after Zenith has been put to bed, I read the latest issue of *In Touch* magazine while soaking in a hot bubble bath.

A few minutes later, Eric enters the bathroom and kneels down to scrub my back with a homemade sugar-based exfoliant he found at the farmer's market last week.

"I'm really proud of you being elected room parent," I tell him. "You don't know how much of an honor it is."

"Sure, I do. I know all about the politics that go into it. I've become an expert after all those years of corporate life. Being room parent will be easy compared with commanding a team of IT experts."

I stare down at the bubbles surrounding my legs, remembering our conversation the other night. "Are you really miserable not working?"

Eric sits down on the toilet and folds his hands. "Honestly? I wouldn't say I'm miserable. Sure, I miss work. I miss breaking things and fixing things and shaking things up. I miss talking shop with others who are like me. I know there are chat rooms, blogs, websites, and news feeds, but it's not the same thing as sitting in a room full of people playing a LAN game during lunch." He scratches the back of his head. "Don't get me wrong. I enjoy parenting and helping out in the classroom. It's different, not better or worse. Just different."

My big toe catches a slow drip from the faucet. "I have a few father's groups you might want to look into for companionship," I say.

He laughs. "If I had time for a father's group."

"I'm sure you could make time. They only meet once a week for an hour or so."

A long moment passes between us. "Okay," Eric says, "I'll look into it."

He stands up to leave, then sits down again. "What about you? Are you upset about working?"

I remember the luxury of sitting in my bath robe after the bus left and sipping my coffee and watching the *Today* show. Now, I shower, dress, and either bike or drive through traffic without a second to think. I remember the variety of running errands, volunteering in Zenith's classroom, lunching with other moms, and exercising at the gym downtown. Now, I spend long hours sitting at the front desk answering phones. I remember the delightful afternoons in the park painting, while Zenith played on the monkey bars. Now, I am too drained to pick up a paint brush. I remember the petty fights with Zenith over homework and the endless worry about when Eric would come home. Now, I come home to find Eric cooking dinner and Zenith's homework already done. Hmm. I guess there are some perks to working.

I think of the gossiping harpies and Emilio's outburst today. "I didn't like it at first," I admit, "but it seems to be growing on me." I think of the extra responsibilities Frank has entrusted me with, and how I seem to be excelling at them.

Eric nods, as if understanding. "It's hard to adjust to working with adults when you're used to dealing with kids."

I sink further into the bubbles until I can no longer see my feet. "At least kids don't think you're stupid."

He nods. "And kids always show you what they're feeling. You always know you're admired and loved for who you are."

Like Frank, I think, drawing circles in the bubbles with my big toe. Just like Frank.

Chapter 12

The next morning there is an orange sticky note on my desk written in Frank's narrow, slanted scrawl. "See me," it says.

I leave the phones on voice mail and head down the aisle toward Frank's office at the back of the bank's administrative offices. The door is closed. I knock three times. I expect to hear him say, "Come in," but the door opens and Frank grabs my hand and pulls me inside.

"Have a seat," he says, closing the door. Soft jazz plays through his computer's speakers.

I perch at the edge of the chair and fold my hands in my lap. Frank stands against his desk. His palms grip the edges and his feet anchor his body to the floor. I wonder what this impromptu meeting is about. Maybe another aberration has been unraveled in the mysterious operations of World Bank.

"When I came into the office this morning, there was a pow wow in the break room," Frank says. "Emilio was at the center of it, dancing and singing, 'Don't hate me because I'm pretty,' and the girls from Accounting were laughing at his skit. When I asked what the song and dance was all about, Emilio told me you were vying for his job. The girls from Accounting were quiet. One of them was so scared; she turned around and threw up in the sink." Frank lowers his voice. "I fired Emilio. I don't have time to shop around for another assistant, so I'm hoping you'll accept my offer to work with me in Emilio's former capacity as my Executive Assistant."

My throat is tight and my hands are dry. Did Frank fire Emilio for parodying me? Is he offering me a promotion? Am I going to be paid more?

"Well, I'm surprised," I stammer.

"Why surprised?"

"Because Emilio was your right-hand-man."

"He's a traitor. He interviewed with World for their marketing position. When he didn't get it, he interviewed for their Executive Assistant position. He was going to leave in two weeks anyway. I've just helped him move along a little quicker."

"But I don't understand why World would be hiring, if they're doing as poorly as we suspect."

"Turnover, babe. When the insiders know something's rotten, they leave. They have to keep their staff replenished, and who better to hire than the competition. Fresh blood."

"Oh." I never thought of it that way. Jeez, I have so much to learn.

"So, what do you say? Will you take the position? The hours are the same. I'll train you on all the responsibilities. And there's a fifty percent raise."

Fifty percent raise? Is he serious? That means I'll be making what Eric used to make working in IT.

"Yes, I'll take it." I'll have the desk right outside Frank's office. I'll no longer have to worry about Jim staring at my breasts when he walks into the office. I'll no longer have to make coffee in the morning or hear the harpies in Accounting gossiping about nonsense. And I get to work directly with Frank. "I'd be honored."

"I got promoted!" I say as soon as I get home that evening.

Eric quickly minimizes the computer screen and swivels around in his chair. "Promoted?"

Zenith jumps up from the sofa where she has been reading a Magic Treehouse book and wraps her arms around my waist. "Does that mean we can go to Disneyland?"

I laugh.

Eric stands up and walks over to me. His eyebrows pinch together in confusion. "What happened to your old job?"

I drop my purse on the coffee table, slip off my heels, and sink down on the sofa. Zenith snuggles up against me. Eric perches on the arm of the loveseat, gaping at me.

I tuck my legs under my hips and smile. "Well, it's a long story," I say, hoping to build a little suspense. "But to make it short, Frank fired his Executive Assistant and hired me. I get a fifty percent raise and get to work for Frank. No more phones, no more mindless projects, no more overhearing pointless gossip. Isn't it great!"

Eric doesn't look a bit excited. In fact, he looks a tad bit concerned. "Are you sure this is great news? Sounds like the guy created an excuse to spend more time with you."

My enthusiasm feels snuffed out like a candle flame. "Really, Eric, why don't you trust Frank? He's only treated me with respect. He's never made a pass at me, or said something offensive or rude or discriminating or harassing. He's a complete gentleman. Why are you so hard on him?"

Eric gazes at Zenith. "Honey, why don't you go into your room and close the door and play with your Polly Pockets till dinner is ready, okay? Mommy and Daddy are going to have an adult conversation."

Zenith frowns at her father, but does not say a word. She turns to me and asks, "Kissy, please?" Without waiting for a response, she lifts her head and puckers her lips.

I bend down and kiss her twice. "We won't talk long," I promise her.

After she has disappeared, Eric joins me on the sofa and wraps his arm around my shoulders like he's trying to protect me from something. His voice is low. "Isn't this a little suspicious, dear? You've only been on the job for three months, and you're being promoted from an entry-level position to a high-level position without any training or education or experience to justify the move. I seriously think this guy is not to be trusted. He's after something else. And I don't mean dictation."

I pout. Eric thinks I'm stupid. Just like Vi thinks I'm stupid. And the women in Accounting. And Emilio. And everyone, except Frank.

Okay, maybe if everyone thinks I'm stupid except Frank, then Frank is wrong and everyone is right. I am stupid. I'm so stupid; I don't know when I'm being setup to be taken advantage of.

But how can that be true? My chest tightens. Am I that gullible? Is my self-esteem so low that it takes an old man in a position of power to make me feel good about myself? Is that why everyone I hold near and dear makes me feel bad, because I'm so depressed about things that I can't see straight anymore?

I stare at my wedding band, a simple gold ring, nothing fancy, and wonder what type of ring Frank's wife wears. Is it a Cartier solitaire or a two carat Tiffany diamond set in white gold? And why do I even care? I'm not romantically interested in Frank. And I'm not envious of his stay-at-home, organic-eating, yogi-stretching wife. Am I? Am I that petty that I'll ruin my marriage over a chance to make something of myself? To prove what? That I'm not dumb? That I can support my family financially? That I can make a difference in the world?

A tear slips from the corner of my eye and dribbles down my cheek. Eric wipes it away with his thumb. He pulls me close and kisses me, first on the cheek, then on the mouth. My body turns instinctively toward him. He places his hands in my hair and massages my scalp, and all the anger, bitterness, disappointment, and envy melts away until all I can feel is his passionate love.

Chapter 13

The next day, I hurry into the office with a brisk skip in my step. My hair has been swept up into a bun, and my lips are painted with pink gloss. I'm wearing my favorite loose-fitting blouse and pencil skirt with my comfy Rockport heels and that damn button advertising Vine Valley's motto, "Bank Better," above my heart. Jim gives me the once over as I pass his office. The women in Accounting stop and stare as I continue walking around the corner and straight back toward Frank's office.

I settle in the standard office swivel chair and survey my new desk. Emilio left nothing behind except the computer, monitor, and phone. There is not even a desk mat, a calendar, a business card holder, or a pen. I take out my sketchbook and pencil and write a list of things I will need to purchase: paper clips, stapler, letter opener, pencils, and pens.

"Hey, babe," Frank says. He carries a bouquet of fall flowers and hands them to me. "It's good to have you on board. I'm glad you decided to be part of my team."

"Thanks for the opportunity," I say, cautiously, remembering Eric's words of warning. I accept the bouquet from Frank. Gosh, these are beautiful. There are orange Asiatic lilies, brick and beige roses, and yellow daisy poms amidst a flourish of greenery. And they smell divine. I can't remember the last time anyone bought me flowers.

"There are vases in the kitchen under the sink," Frank says. He taps the desk with his fingertips. "Don't worry about the office supplies. I'll have Jim order whatever you need."

Frank disappears into his office and shuts the door.

I sniff the perfume of the heavenly bouquet and hustle to the break room to find a vase. Two women from Accounting stand in front of the coffee machine. They turn and gape at the bouquet in my hands.

"Who bought you flowers?"

"The bank," I say, "to celebrate my promotion."

One of the women narrows her eyes at me. "You mean the job you stole from Emilio."

I bend to search beneath the sink for a vase. "Emilio left to work for World Bank," I say. I find a ceramic cinnamon-colored vase with hand-painted gold leaves and fill it with water. I arrange the flowers carefully, plucking a bent leaf off a beige rose.

The woman who made the rude comment leaves. The other woman continues to stand beside me. For a moment, I can't remember her name. Toni? No, it's Romi. She works as the Controller and drives a new BMW. She wears a smart emerald green sweater dress with cuffed sleeves decorated with brassy buttons and sleek stockings and ankle boots. Her freshly painted face matches the colors of the bouquet, from her amber-colored eyes to her ruddy lips. She sips her mug of coffee, and a wave of her auburn hair curls beneath her chin. She gazes at me solemnly, studying me for clues as to why I would be offered the promotion instead of the bank hiring someone else, someone more qualified. My lower back tightens against her silent judgment.

"I know what you think," I say, "and it's not true. I'm not just a pretty face."

A snicker flickers across Romi's attractive face. She sips her coffee and smiles slowly. "I admire your spunk. I wouldn't want to work directly with Frankie. He's very demanding from what Emilio shared with us."

"He's also very respectful and appreciative." I clutch the bouquet and narrow my eyes at her. "He expects the best from his employees, and if that means he's very demanding, then so be it. I can meet the challenge."

The woman lifts her eyebrows. "I'm not saying you can't," she says. "I just hope you know what you're getting into and that you're doing it for the right reasons."

"Why do you even care?" I snap.

Her amber eyes seem to dim against the sharpness of my comment. Her voice is soft, almost kind. "Because I was once like you," she says. "And I didn't know what I was getting into." She whispers, "I ended up almost drowning."

I don't know if she feels compassion or pity for me, and frankly, I don't care. I hold her gaze, feeling my resolve grow. "Don't worry about me," I say. "I know how to swim."

Oh, God, please help me make it through the day.

It's only nine o'clock and already Frank has pulled me into his office to brief me on his day. There are meetings scheduled every two hours with one department or another or one bank or another, or one prospective client or another. Already, my sketchbook holds more words than pictures.

I am supposed to check the e-mails Frank forwards me so I know everything that he knows. I figure I'll be here for a while, so I make a cup of mint tea and settle into my new space. The e-mails start to download into Outlook, until I have received all 1,968 messages.

I scroll down and read the subject lines quickly, before starting at the bottom and moving up. There are messages from the Loan Operations Manager, the Credit Administration Manager, the New Accounts Manager, the Branch Managers, and a dozen non-profit organizations we support as part of our "Local Bank Does the Community Good" campaign designed by the marketing staff. Nothing seems too outrageously important, until I get to an e-mail from Buddy from World Bank. It just says, "Call me."

Hmm. I sip my tea and wonder why the mysterious message. Has World decided to accept our pennies on the dollar offer, or are they trying to bargain for more since their publicity department has done such a fabulous job of convincing the public that they are stronger than their financial records show?

My phone rings. "Hey, babe, I have Buddy on the phone. Can you come in and take notes? Bring the laptop."

I leave my tea on the desk and carry the laptop into Frank's office. In the background, turned down so low you can barely hear it, Bush sings, "Everything Zen." On Frank's bookshelf, I notice photos of a stunningly beautiful woman with wavy golden blond hair wearing a hemp dress and a twine bracelet and no makeup. She looks to be a little older than me, or maybe that's just because there are crow's feet around her hazel eyes. I wonder if she is Frank's wife.

"Yeah, Buddy, I have Bev in here with me to take notes, if you don't mind."

"Not at all," he chuckles. "You remember me, Bev?"

"Of course, I do," I say, trying to keep it as professional as possible. The laptop springs to life and I pull up a blank document and save it as "Notes" with the date. My fingers poise over the home keys, ready to type.

Frank and Buddy start to jabber back and forth at record speed. My fingers try to keep up, but I'm not sure what to type. Do I include all the umms and ahhs? How to I keep each person's comments straight? Why didn't I take Modern Dictation in college, instead of The Science of Superheroes? At the time, I thought it was much more educational than Eric's History of Cyberporn, but now I know it was a complete waste of time. After all, who needs to know the theory of fluid dynamics by watching video clips of Superman flying? Honestly, I would have been better served by enrolling in Business Basics. Oh, well.

By the time their conversation is over, I've written and saved about half of what was said and in no logical order. I figure I'll have time to type it up nicely later, but Frank says we need to prepare for his ten o'clock meeting, which means I am off to the front desk to gather information that has been sent overnight. Jim sits at my old desk looking frustrated and glum, but his head jolts upright when he sees me approaching.

"Well, well, well, have you come for your old job?"

"Umm, no, actually, I'm here for a FedEx package for Frank."

Jim rummages through the Will Call pile until he finds the slim envelope. I sign for it and catch Jim staring at my "Bank Better" button. I try not to frown, placing the envelope firmly against my chest and turning away.

At my desk, I sink down into the chair and open up the envelope. I reach over to take a sip of tea, but it's cold. The envelope inside says, *Confidential*, in big block letters. Should I open it? Or give it to Frank to open?

I wander into the break room to make a fresh cup of tea. Romi stands over the table, scanning the headlines. She glances up at me and smiles, "How is your first day going?"

"Wonderful," I say, dunking my tea bag into fresh hot water.

"Glad to hear it," Romi says.

She wants me to fail, I think. They all do. But I'll show them. I'll master this job one way or the other.

As soon as I sit down and pick up the confidential envelope, Frank buzzes me. "I have Clark Peterson from Peterson Bakery on the line and I want you to join us. He's a big potential client I've been trying to secure. It would be great if we could refinance all his commercial properties."

I grab the laptop and shuttle back into Frank's office and open up another blank document and type "Peterson Bakery" with the date and save the document. This time, I skip over the umms and ahhs and record only the meat and potatoes of the conversation. I use C for Clark and F for Frank, and resist adding B for myself when I make a comment about how much Zenith loves Peterson Bakery's famous cinnamon apple turnovers filled with real whipped cream and doused with powdered sugar on top. Mmm. Just thinking of them makes me hungry and it's not even nine-thirty.

By the time Mr. Peterson agrees to meet with Frank to discuss transferring his bank accounts, my fingers ache from typing so much. This must be how musicians feel when they're just learning how to play an instrument. I wonder how much practice I must have before my fingers become dexterous.

I return to my desk to tackle the confidential letter and reach for my cup of tea. It's cold again. A quick glance at the clock on my computer alerts me to the fact that I have nine minutes to prepare for Frank's ten o'clock meeting. I resist making another cup of tea and open up the confidential envelope and scan the contents. It's from the FDIC and it looks rather important. Hmm. There's something about failed banks and buyout offers and some reference to telephone conversations and e-mails that go back before I even started working here. I make a photocopy and hand Frank the original.

"What does it say?" he asks.

Am I supposed to interpret documents? Somehow, I didn't imagine it was part of the job description, but apparently it is.

"It's from the FDIC," I say. "They want you to know they are prepared to approve the buyout of World Bank."

"Excellent," Frank says, taking the letter from my hand. He scans the letter and smiles. "You know, this is almost reason to celebrate."

"It is?"

He nods. "If World won't accept our offer, they'll be seized by the FDIC and given to us." He snaps his fingers. "Just like that."

"Really?" I sink down into the chair across from him.

He turns back to his computer monitor and prints out a spreadsheet. "This is what we're worth and this is what World is worth." Frank jabs his fingers at the final number. "And this is what we will be worth once we buyout World Bank."

I stare at the number: $58 billion.

"That's not much," Frank reassures me. "The average national bank is worth about $129 billion. But it's a start."

Wow. $58 billion. I can't even imagine that much money. Would it stack up to Pluto and back? Or would it only go as far as Saturn?

The phone rings. "Frank, here. Yes, Jim, put him through."

Frank nods for me to take notes. I open up the laptop and begin to type, but my thoughts keep coming back to $58 billion. No wonder Frank can afford my raise. He's a billionaire.

Okay, maybe he's not a billionaire, but the bank is. Or will be. Once this deal closes.

"Did you get that, Bev?" Frank asks.

"Hmm." I glance up and realize I've missed a part of the conversation by daydreaming about money. Oh, no. I hope it wasn't important.

"Steve just gave us the direct number for the Office of the Comptroller of Currency. Can you read it back to me?"

Oh, no. I can't. I absolutely didn't hear it. Any of it.

"Uh."

Frank presses his fingertips together in the shape of a pyramid and says, "Steve, do you mind giving us that number again?" Frank gazes at me meaningfully.

This time I type it down and repeat it back for confirmation.

By the time the conversation ends, perspiration drips down the back of my neck. I must reek. Frank immediately turns up the volume of his music. Ozzy sings "Scream." For once, it's appropriate. I want to scream, and I'm sure Frank does, too, for hiring me for a job I am obviously not qualified to perform. But Frank does not say a word. I pack up the laptop and head out of the office, closing the door quietly as I leave.

At my desk, I glance at the blinking light on my phone and wonder who could be calling me. It must be a message for Emilio. I sit down, press play, and listen. Sure enough, it is a woman calling to reschedule a lunch date. "Tell Frankie I won't be able to make it," she says in a breathy voice. "He'll understand."

I play back the message again, trying to hear a name or a call back number. Obviously, she does not know I do not recognize her voice. I haven't had time to change the outgoing message.

What should I do? What if it's a psycho woman who has been stalking Frank? No, not likely. Psycho people don't normally leave messages.

Okay. Maybe it's a sister or a college friend.

No, not likely. Not with that breathless Marilyn Monroe voice.

Well, then, I guess it must be. . . a secret lover. Why else would she not leave a name or a number?

My stomach twists into a knot. Oh, my. Eric was right. Frank flatters and beds women. He must have a whole bunch of them. Like a collection. I wonder how many other phone calls like this I will receive. Emilio must have been the go-between, screening their calls and shielding them from the knowledge of his wife.

Bastard.

Well, if that's the way he likes to play, I will let him know I cannot be an accomplice. I will resign. Surely, Jim will give me back my old position.

I pick up the phone and buzz Frank.

"Yeah, babe," he says.

All right, I think. I can do this. It's no different than confronting a friend with the ugly truth. "A woman left a message for you. No name, no number. She's canceling lunch."

There is a long pause before Frank says, "That's my wife."

"Oh." Of course, I think. It's not like Frank has a secret lover or anything, right?

I can't believe for a moment I thought that he might. Jeez, I feel as bad as a stupid housewife believing everyone has something hidden and unknown about themselves that they can't wait to reveal on reality TV.

I hang up the phone, grab my mug of tea, and nearly spit out the cold liquid. Eek. It tastes terrible. I set the mug down and unlock my computer and start reading the e-mails Frank sent over this morning.

A few minutes later, Frank emerges from his office. He stops in front of me, his fingers poised at the edge of my desk. I hunch forward. I wish I had a pair of sunglasses I could hide behind like a poker player, but I don't.

"Holding up, babe?" he asks.

"I'm fine." I glance up at him and smile brightly, although I feel absolutely withered inside.

"Since my wife canceled our date at Organic Bistro, I'm headed home to surprise her." He glances at his watch. "Cancel my one o'clock, okay? But I'll be back in time for my two-thirty."

How sweet. He's going home to surprise his wife. How rotten of me to think he was cheating on her.

When he's gone, I make the Sign of the Cross and whisper, "Please, God, forgive me for doubting Frank. And help me to learn to do my job right ASAP."

Chapter 14

On Friday, after work, I arrive home to chaos. The sofa, loveseat, and coffee table are pushed back against the walls. Zenith and Mindi are spread out in sleeping bags with a small mountain of toys surrounding them like a fortress. Eric sits at the computer working on something. As soon as I shut the door, he minimizes the screen and pulls up a news feed to make it look like he was doing nothing other than keeping up with current events.

My heartbeat thumps in my chest and my legs feel weak. Not again. Please, God, let him not be working on something that's illegal, immoral, or just plain foolish. I haven't had a chance to worry about what's happening at home with everything that has been going on at work. Now that it's Friday with the prospect of two days to relax, the pressure of work has been released, only to start mounting again with Eric's quick cover up of whatever little project he's been working on while I make money to pay our bills.

"Hi, Mommy!"

"Hi, Mrs. Mael!"

"Hello, girls!" I stoop down to hug and kiss them amidst all of their stuff.

Well, mostly it's Mindi's stuff. It looks like she carts most of her stuff between her mother's townhouse and her father's condo.

Oh, well. It's only one night.

"How was your day?" Eric asks, logging off of the computer.

I shrug. "Fine. Everything's fine."

It's not fine. It's far from fine. I haven't gotten used to anything yet. From the flurry of e-mails that bombard me each day, to the endless list of tasks Frank expects me to do, to the boring meetings I must transcribe, and everything in between, I am absolutely overwhelmed and exhausted. Frank asked to see my sketchbook yesterday and I reluctantly handed it over to him. He flipped through the pages and frowned. "You haven't been drawing," he said.

"I haven't had time," I replied.

He studied the blank wall above my desk. "You know, we need a painting in here. Why don't you hang one of your paintings above the desk? Personalize your space a bit. You'll be spending a lot of time here. I want you to feel like you're at home."

Jeez, as if I had nothing else to do on my day off but paint.

But I don't tell Eric any of this. I pretend everything is going well. I do not want him or anyone else to badger me about my new position, to say my struggles are proof that I am not qualified for the job, that my boss has ulterior motives for hiring me, that I am nothing but a pretty face.

The buzzer rings in the kitchen. The girls jump up and shout in unison, "Pizza's ready!"

Eric pulls me close for a quick hug and a grope before heading off to the kitchen. I pad down the hallway and into our bedroom, shut the door, and change out of my work clothes and into a baggy gray T-shirt and soft yoga pants. Eric's laptop is open on the mattress. I tiptoe over and glance at the screen. Damn. It's locked. Well, what else did I expect? For him to leave everything open for anyone to see?

I wonder what he's working on and I wonder when he'll tell me. If he'll tell me.

By the time I return to the kitchen, the homemade pizza smells of garlic and basil and mozzarella cheese. I sit down and wait for everyone before making the Sign of the Cross and saying grace. The comfort of the cradling chair and the familiar chatter of the girls lull me into a daze. My eyes feel sore and my arms feel heavy. I blink several times and consider making a cup of coffee just to get through the next couple of hours before I can slip into bed to sleep.

Several conversations later, none of which I was paying any particular attention to, Eric mentions the homemade sundaes we'll be making for dessert. "I picked up some of that hard shell chocolate coating for you, Bev," he says. "I know you always loved getting those when we could afford to go to the Freeze. And it was on sale."

"Did you pick up any decorations for the party yet?" Zenith asks.

"I'm ordering everything online for twenty percent off and free shipping," Eric says. "And we're getting our costumes online, too. Are you dressing up, Bev?" He gazes at me with interest, and I try to stifle a yawn.

"Dunno," I say. "I haven't had time to think about it."

"You could be a ladybug, like me," Zenith says.

"Or a genie, like me," says Mindi.

"Or a scary clown, like me." Eric flashes an evil grin.

I glance around the table, suddenly feeling left out. How did I get so preoccupied and worn out with work that I no longer know or care what is going on in my own family?

I rub my forehead. Maybe I should go make a cup of coffee. At least I'll perk up then. "Maybe I'll be a movie star," I say. "It's easy. I'll wear big sunglasses and carry a sign that says, No Paparazzi."

"No, Mommy, you have to be something different than who you are," Zenith says.

"I'm not a movie star."

Mindi studies me. "But you look like a movie star."

Even the kids think I'm just a pretty face. "Fine," I say, tearing off another piece of pizza. "I'll be an ugly wicked witch with a green face and a wart on her nose."

Everyone cheers like it's the greatest thing I've said all week.

Maybe, I think, it is.

While the girls are making their ice cream sundaes, Eric's cell phone beeps.

"Who is it?" I ask.

He takes the phone out of his pocket and checks the text message. "It's Lori. She's asking about the Halloween party."

He types a response and shoves the phone in his pocket and loads the dishwasher. The girls sit at the kitchen table eating their sundaes. I scoop vanilla ice cream into a bowl and pour the chocolate syrup on top and watch it harden.

Eric's phone beeps again.

He takes out his phone, glances at the message, and shakes his head. "She's so annoying. She wants everything to be perfect. Doesn't she understand that all the kids care about is having fun?"

I remember Lori. From her colored hair to her manicured toes, she is absolutely perfect. "She lives her life through her children," I say. "This party is huge for her. She must feel like a part of her is dying because she can't organize it."

Eric shrugs and turns off his phone. "I don't care. I can't be on call for a school party. It's unreasonable." He starts the dishwasher and towel dries his hands. "I don't know how you did it, putting up with those crazy housewives every single day, every single school year. It's just amazing what these women are like." He takes a bowl down from the cabinet and fills it with strawberry ice cream. "They talk about the most inconsequential things. Like who is doing what in *Real Housewives*." He shakes his head. "*They're* the real housewives. Why can't they talk about that instead?"

I move closer to him and put my hand on his back. "I'm sure Zenith appreciates the sacrifice."

His eyes light up. "Oh, the kids love me. And I love them. It's the moms I can't stand."

I purse my lips. "Have you thought about joining a father's group?"

"Yeah, it's on my list of things to do." He grabs a can of whipped cream and decorates the top of my chocolate-covered vanilla cream with a swirling top hat. "Ta-da," he says. "It's not great art like your paintings, but it's my art and it's edible."

"Mmm, my favorite kind." I put a spoonful in my mouth.

After dessert, we retire to the living room to watch *Cloudy with a Chance of Meatballs*. I sit on the loveseat next to Eric with my feet propped up on the ottoman. He wraps his arm around the back of the seat and rests his broad hand on my shoulder. His skin is warm and soothing. I snuggle closer to him and rest my head against his shoulder.

Halfway through the movie, my eyelids droop and my head bobs back. I jolt awake at the shock of cool, sticky whipped cream sprayed in my open mouth. The girls squeal with laughter. Eric chuckles. In the flicker of the TV, I notice the can of whipped cream in Eric's hand. I stand up and stagger to the kitchen sink and rinse my mouth with warm water.

Eric follows me into the kitchen. His body trembles with laughter. "You should have seen your face."

"Before or after you sprayed me with whipped cream?"

"Both." He chuckles.

I can't believe he thinks this is funny. That he thinks everything is funny. I stalk past him. "Goodnight, girls," I say. "Mommy's tired."

"Night," they say in unison.

"Ah, c'mon," Eric says, chasing me down the hall. "Where's your sense of humor?"

I spin around at our bedroom's threshold. "I don't have one right now. I'm tired."

Eric studies my face. The faint snicker creasing his mouth disappears. "You're just like them."

"What are you talking about?"

"The moms. I understand how you got along with them. You're just like them. You don't have a sense of humor."

Some part of me crumples like a wad of paper inside. "Everything with you is a joke," I say.

"You have to admit, spraying whipped cream in your mouth while you're dozing is pretty funny."

In spite of my overwhelming fatigue, a smile flickers across my face. "You're right," I say. "It was pretty funny."

Eric traces the circles under my eyes with his fingertip. "And you're right, too," he says. "You're pretty tired." He pulls me close and holds me tight. "Get some sleep. I'll take care of the girls, okay?"

A tear dribbles silently down my cheek. Maybe Eric's right. My sense of humor has fizzled along with my energy. Ever since I accepted the position as Frank's Executive Assistant, I have been working so much, I barely remember my own name. But I'm too proud to give up. I have too much to prove to everyone.

Chapter 15

I wake the next morning to Eric getting dressed in a. . .suit?

I sit up and squint in the sunlight. "Where are you going?" Does he have a job interview on a Saturday?

Eric smiles sheepishly. "Sorry. I didn't mean to wake you. I've been trying to be quiet." He ties a striped turquoise and white tie around his neck. I remember going with Zenith to Kohl's to pick it out for Father's Day a few years ago. He only wears it on special occasions. "I have a meeting this morning with Mike Russell. I told you about it last night at dinner, but I think you were too tired to hear."

I draw my legs up to my chest and rest my cheek on my knees. "Isn't Mike an attorney? Are you in some sort of trouble I should know about?"

Eric laughs. He sits on the edge of the mattress and ruffles my hair. "No, sweetheart, I am not in any trouble. Mike's an intellectual property attorney now. He stopped practicing criminal law when Judge Stewart was elected, remember? I just want to go over a few things with him. I've been working on a project and want to know what it will take to license my software."

What type of software has Eric been writing? I thought it was just that prank to break into PG&E. Sure, he said he was working on a few things, but he never mentioned anything serious. Especially not something with the potential to generate an income.

Eric kisses my forehead and stands up to inspect his reflection. He has shaved the stubble from his chin and sprayed that musky cologne Zenith bought him for Father's Day that smells as cheap as it is. I wish I had the money to buy him something better. The suit is a tiny bit tight across the back and shoulders from the amount of muscle mass he's put on over the months, but overall, he looks as handsome as the day I asked him if he wanted to try the Code Red Mountain Dew my father had bought for the store.

"If I can successfully license the software to a big name company, then you can be a stay-at-home mom again. And I can be the working man." He winks.

Does he really expect me to stay home after all the progress I've been making at work? Or does he suspect I'm going to fail him and embarrass the whole family? Or is this about something else? His ambition? His pride? Was this what he meant when he said this is who he is and nothing can change it? That he had to write this software whether or not it goes anywhere? Hmm. I think that must be it.

"Good luck," I say.

"Thanks. The girls are still sleeping, but I've put all the ingredients for making pancakes on the counter. I should be back before lunch."

He opens the bedroom door.

"Eric?"

He turns toward me, lifting his eyebrows. "Yes?"

A slow smile spreads across my face. "I'm proud of you."

His face flushes bright pink before he leaves, closing the door behind him.

It's a half hour before church and Eric has not returned home. I have tried calling him, but he does not answer.

The girls and I have spent the day making pancakes, hiking around Vine Valley Lake, making sandwiches and sundaes, and playing Monopoly for two hours. Mindi has her sleeping bag and overnight bag stowed in the trunk of the Ford Escort and the girls are anxious to leave.

"Go ahead," I tell the girls, "I'll meet you in the car."

I type a quick text to Eric and leave my phone on vibrate.

Out of Balance

At church, the girls march ahead of me holding hands, their dark heads tilted toward one another. For a moment, I think they could be sisters, and I feel a sweet thankfulness they have each other.

Inside the cathedral with its high dome ceiling and stained glass windows depicting the lives of saints, I dip my fingers in holy water and make the Sign of the Cross. Mindi and Zenith have found a spot near the front by the altar and are kneeling down to pray. I scan the dimly lit room, searching for Bob, but I don't see him.

I walk up to the big red book splayed open on a podium before the center aisle and pick up a pen and write down my special intentions for the week—to learn how to do my job, to discover what is going on with Eric, and to keep my thoughts pure.

"Well, well, well, if it isn't Business Barbie. Where's Mr. Clean?"

I drop the pen and spin around. A short, fat man with a bushel of blond hair greets me with a hug. Bob is wearing a red Ralph Lauren polo shirt and black Calvin Klein slacks and John Lobb suede shoes, and smells of too much spicy Pasha de Cartier cologne. But his bear hug seems to relieve some of the tension built up from Eric being gone all day. It's not that I don't like spending the whole day with the girls; it's that I don't like spending the whole day without Eric.

"Where are the little munchkins?" Bob asks.

I point toward the altar. Zenith and Mindi sit on the pew with their heads close together, whispering.

Bob smiles and nods. "They're like little angels in church. Too bad they can't be that way all the time."

"They're not that bad," I say.

"They giggle all the time," says Bob. "I don't remember finding everything funny when I was their age."

"No, but I'm sure Eric did," I tell him.

"Where is Mr. Clean anyway?"

I wish Bob wouldn't call us by the names of toys, cartoons, or brand name characters. "He said he'd meet us at church."

Bob studies my face for a long moment. "Don't worry, Barbie. It's not like he's cheating on you." He shakes his head sadly. "It's a shame men can't find mistresses that come halfway close to looking like you. Most mistresses are uglier than wives, but listen better. Fat people listen well; they have to. They don't have much else to offer."

I wonder if the older woman Bob left Vi for is fat and a good listener. Bob never mentions the older woman, and some part of me wonders if the older woman story Vi told me was just an excuse to get me to stop asking questions when she filed for divorce.

"Want to join us?" I ask.

Bob follows me down the aisle and slides next to me in the pew. When Mindi notices him, she bounces up and scoots across to sit next to him. Zenith gets up and wedges past me and Bob to sit next to Mindi. I'm left at the end of the pew. I place my purse beside me, saving a spot for Eric, if he decides to show up.

Just before the pianist plays, "All Are Welcome," Eric bustles up the side aisle, picks up my purse, and sits down beside me. He kisses my cheek. "Sorry I'm late," he whispers.

I want to ask him how the meeting went, but we've been asked to stand and sing the opening greeting.

Halfway through mass, Eric takes out his phone and starts to type. I nudge him with my elbow and he flashes me a mischievous grin. "God's talking to me," he says. "I need to take notes."

It's not that I don't believe God talks to Eric. The few times Eric has confided in me about his conversations with God, the predictions God made all came true. Like the collapse of Lehman Brothers and, more personally, the death of both of Eric's parents. I just wish God would text him instead.

By the time we file out of the pew to receive Communion, I've forgotten all about the anger and frustration I've been feeling at work and the anxiety and worry I've been feeling at home. The pianist and guitarist that make up our two person choir play, "On Eagles Wings," my favorite song, and I sing the words, letting my breath swell in my chest, my hands clasped in prayer, my eyes focused on the resurrected Jesus.

After Mass, we file out into the parking lot. The sun has almost set, leaving the sky a brilliant blood red. In the distance, a honey-colored moon starts to rise, and I remember the evening I spent with Eric in the Home Depot parking lot watching the moon rise before the lights of the city blacked out. My thoughts wander to Eric's meeting with Mike Russell, but Eric is busy talking with Bob about Bob's insurance business, the repairs Bob made to his house on the lake, and whether or not Bob will make it to the class field trip to Arnold's Pumpkin Patch next week.

While Bob and Eric talk and Mindi and Zenith hug, I load Mindi's overnight bag and sleeping bag in the trunk of Bob's Mercedes. I glance at my watch, wondering how soon I can call Vi to ask about her date with the MyMate.com doctor. I decide I can't wait any longer and send her a text, "How did your date go?" A couple of minutes later, my phone beeps. I read the message. "The date is still going. Talk to you during the week." I shove my phone into my purse. That must be some doctor. Vi must really like him if she's letting him stay over another night.

Eric finally shakes Bob's hand. Mindi gets into the Mercedes. We watch them drive away. Zenith asks Eric if she can drive home with him. "Sure, honey," he says, opening the door for her.

"Wait," I say, before Eric can get in and drive away. "How did your meeting go?"

Eric leans on the car door and gazes thoughtfully at me. "It didn't go as well as I would have liked," he says. "I thought Mike could negotiate a deal with another company to test my product confidentially even if I had to pay them a fee, but they aren't interested. It seems that they think the product is overdone and not needed in the market, and I couldn't convince them otherwise without exposing myself."

"What are you talking about? What product?" The only product I've seen is the Break-Into-PG&E-and-Turn-Off-the-City's-Lights product.

Eric shakes his head. "You wouldn't understand, okay?"

"Try me."

"Every time I tell you about my work, you get upset."

"C'mon, Eric, how many husbands have work that involves breaking into another company's computer system?"

"Husbands who work for penetration companies, that's who," he says.

I think he's not going to tell me, that he's going to leave me in suspense, anxious and worried over all the possible products he could be creating and all the horrible mischief that might result, especially if he has to get an attorney involved. But he lifts my chin until my eyes are level with his, and my heart starts thumping in my chest.

"You know that stunt I pulled last weekend?"

I nod. How can I forget? The newspaper reporters still write about the mysterious blackout and how PG&E cannot confirm how it happened, only that "measures are being taken to prevent a future occurrence."

"Well, that was only the beginning," Eric says. "I wanted to test how easy it was to break through a firewall without being detected. Then, I wanted to develop a firewall that was so strong that not even I could penetrate it. That's the real project I've been working on. Only I can't show everyone how badly my product is needed without upsetting you, because I know you'd flip out and divorce me if I told everyone I was the person responsible for last weekend's blackout."

He's right. Not necessarily about the divorce part, but the flipping out part.

"Okay, I understand," I say. "But, how can you get your product accepted, if no one knows it's needed?"

Eric taps his phone. "That's where God comes in. I have to trust He knows what He's doing by asking me to contact Black Magic."

"Who's Black Magic?"

Eric squints at me. "It's the biggest underground society of hackers in the Western hemisphere."

"God told you to contact them?" I ask. Why would God refer Eric to an illegal cult?

"It could be my big break into network security," Eric explains.

"Why would a bunch of hackers help you?"

"They might want what I have to offer."

"Which is?"

"A challenge." Eric's eyes flash with delight. "Hackers live for a challenge."

Chapter 16

Okay. Don't panic. My husband is not joining a cult. He's just contacting a bunch of mischief makers to see if they can break through the product he's devised.

Not a problem. Really. I shouldn't even think about it.

But, of course, that's all I think about the rest of the weekend. Even when Eric tells me to clear out the kitchen and setup my easel and paint while he and Zenith go grocery shopping.

I take out my concerns on the canvas with a palate knife full of bold acrylic paint. I slash the white canvas with yellow ochre, burnt sienna, and flaming crimson, creating an abstract masterpiece full of autumnal fire, expressing the End of the World worry I feel, but am otherwise unable to articulate.

"Wow! I think that's your best painting yet," Eric says when he gets home.

He sets the bag of groceries on the kitchen counter and stands with his hands on his waist, studying the painting. "I think you should enter it at the Harvest Fair next weekend."

I sigh. "It's too late to submit an entry. Last weekend was the deadline."

"Are you sure?" Eric asks.

I nod. Each year I've always thought about entering a painting, but I've always chickened out at the last minute. This year, I've been so consumed with work that I've completely forgotten about fantasizing about entering the annual competition.

"Maybe I'll talk to the committee next week," Eric says. "See if they can make an exception."

"Who do you know on the committee?"

"Katy Louis, Valerie's mom. She owes me a favor for jump starting her car last week so she wouldn't be late to Girl Scouts."

I never understood the I-scratch-your-back, you-scratch-mine philosophy. But if it works for Eric, fine.

"It's worth a shot," Eric says, kissing my cheek. "That painting's too good to sit in our bedroom closet. The whole world needs to see it."

On Monday morning, Frank strolls down the hallway whistling "Seek and Destroy" by Metallica. He sets a stack of papers on my desk and says, "I need the statistics from Accounting as soon as possible for my nine o'clock meeting." He swaggers into his office and closes the door.

I pull up my e-mails and check the messages on my phone, before going to the kitchen to make a cup of mint tea. While pushing the button for hot water on the dispenser, I glance at the headlines. "PG&E terminates IT Manager for alleged foul play." I wonder if that poor manager was fired for Eric's exploit. "Ow!" Hot water splashes against my foot. I release the button and wince. Water sloshes dangerously against the rim of my mug. I place the mug on the table and hop to the sink to soak some paper towels in cold water.

"Here, let me help you," Romi says, taking an ice pack down from the freezer and wrapping it with a cloth towel from one of the drawers.

I feel my face flush as hot as my foot feels.

"Don't worry," Romi says. "I've done it before. Lots of times." She hands the ice pack to me and bends to wipe up the mess on the floor.

I sit down at the table and prop my foot up on a chair and place the ice pack on the top of my scalded foot.

"I have a better idea," Romi says. "Come to my office and do that. I have comfy chairs and I can give you the statistics your boss needs for his meeting."

I hobble down the hallway following her to a plush office across from the Accounting cubicles where the women are gossiping about their weekends and the upcoming Harvest Fair, and the board meeting next week. Romi leads me to the two plush upholstered chairs facing her massive desk. I sit down on one chair, prop my foot on the other, and gaze longingly out the plexiglass window, wondering how long it took her to work her way up from one of the cubicles to this private office.

She shuts the door and sits down on her leather executive chair and taps at her keyboard. Her auburn hair is pulled away from her porcelain face painted in soft autumn hues. Every now and then, her amber eyes flicker toward me. Her mouth twitches a few times, and I wonder if she's contemplating how to say something that's seriously important in a way she thinks I'll understand.

My foot eventually feels less like molten lava and more like an iceberg. I remove the ice pack and set my foot on the floor. "Do you have the paperwork?" I ask.

"Just a minute," Romi says, clicking through a few more screens. "I wanted to talk to you about your boss before you leave. There are a few things you should know."

I slump against the chair. Not another lecture about Frank and his salacious ways. "He's never made a pass at me," I tell Romi.

"He's not going to," Romi says, her eyes flashing with annoyance. "He's going to wait until you fall in love with him, and then he'll pounce."

What is she talking about? "I'm married. I don't go around falling in love with other men."

"Neither did I," Romi says. "But that didn't stop me from falling for Frank when I was just an intern and he was just a loan officer. We were both married, he to his first wife, and I to my one and only husband. It was just a fling, he said, after it happened, but I thought it would last. Both our marriages broke up. His, because he was never home, and mine, because I had been unfaithful. It was ten years ago, but people don't change." She stops typing and leans across the desk. "I came to this bank with something to prove, and all I ended up with is losing the love of my life and my self-respect. Sure,

I have a posh office and drive a new BMW and live in a luxurious mansion near the golf course, but I'm lonely. I can't make friends with the women I supervise. They're a bunch of petty gossips. I don't have time to socialize. I bring work home. And last week, when I saw that same hardened look of determination on your face, I knew I had to say something to warn you, or I would not be able to live with myself."

Gosh, she looks scary with her flaring nostrils. I don't know what to say.

Romi reaches across the desk and extends her hand as a peace offering. Her immaculate French manicured nails and glitzy gold bracelets and Chanel suit lure me with the fruits of her labor, and I find myself drawn more to her appearance than I am to her words.

"Be careful," she says. "I know you're smart. You found the discrepancies in the general ledger that no one else could find. But don't sacrifice the things you love for the respect you feel you will gain by proving yourself to the world. It's not worth it."

I reluctantly take her hand. She curls her fingers around my palm and squeezes it. Her mouth tightens into a firm line. When she releases my hand, she clicks her mouse and the pages I have come for spit out of the printer.

The warm paper seems to melt against my skin after holding the ice pack for so long. I stand up to leave. Romi stands up also.

"I hope I wasn't too forward with you," she says. "No one at the bank knows my history. Frank and I are the only ones left from that time. The rest moved on to other banks and other opportunities. I trust you can keep this a secret. I wouldn't want the past to become the present again."

I nod, understanding too well the way one comment becomes biblical in the bank. Romi's sad eyes match her sad smile, and for a moment, I want to reach out and hug her, but I don't know if that would be either professional or appropriate. I just can't imagine someone as intelligent and glamorous as her being lonely. If I had the gumption, I would tell her to log onto MyMate.com and post a profile for a date. I'm sure she would have tons of responses. But, after a few seconds, I realize that's not what she's after. She wants what she once had. And that's impossible for anyone to return to her.

"Thanks," I say, "for everything."

Back at my desk, I try to imagine Frank seducing Romi, or Romi seducing Frank. Soon my thoughts are jumbled with sexual positions of the two of them in the server room, the file room, and the vault.

Frank buzzes me. "Are those reports ready?"

"Yes, sir."

I knock once on his door before he tells me to come inside. I step into the office and hear the strains of a violin playing through his speakers.

"Is that Mozart?" I ask.

He takes the papers from my hand and nods. "Baby Mozart to be exact. My wife is six months pregnant and wants to educate our child before he or she is born. So I've been instructed to listen to Baby Mozart instead of my usual rock and roll and occasional jazz."

"Congratulations! Is this your first child?"

He eyes me suspiciously. "Yes, it is. You have children, right?"

"One child. A girl. She's eight."

"If we have a daughter, my wife wants to name her Judi in memory of Judi Bari, the environmentalist and co-founder of Earth First. I prefer something not so historically linked." He leans back and props his legs on the desk, crossing his feet at the ankles. "How did you and your husband decide on your daughter's name?"

I take a seat and fold my hands in my lap, remembering the night Eric and I stood on the balcony of our apartment a week before we were going to move into our house. The stars were out, and Eric rubbed my belly and asked the baby what she saw in our future, and I gazed up into the sky and said, "She sees the zenith." Eric laughed. It became our private joke. Whenever one of us would look up into the night sky and see a star directly overhead, we would say, "It's our daughter, Zenith."

But after my conversation with Romi, I no longer feel comfortable telling Frank something so personal.

"I think you should get a baby book of names and decide on something you both like," I suggest instead.

"Is that what you and your husband did?" Frank gazes at me intently, unafraid of pursuing his original question.

The softness in his eyes melts my resolve. "No, we didn't," I say. "My husband is a jokester. Our daughter's name is the result of a joke."

Frank studies me intently. "I didn't know you had a sense of humor," he says. "You're always so serious."

"It's because I want to be taken seriously," I say.

"Don't worry, babe. You are."

Babe. I never paid any attention to the nickname before, since I assumed he called every woman babe, but now I wonder, am I the only one? I have never heard him address anyone else by that name, not even his wife.

Maybe I'm just being overly concerned, especially after Romi's terrifying confession. The thought of their affair rattles me. I get up to leave. I have plenty of work to do.

Frank's voice hits my back before I've closed the door behind me. "I don't want to name the baby Judi."

I peer at him closely. He looks small and helpless, like a little boy forced to play a game he has no interest in playing. But that's none of my business, right? I'm paid to work for the bank, not fix Frank's personal problems. "Don't tell me," I say with an edge to my voice. "Tell your wife."

That night I can't get any rest. When I finally fall asleep around two, I dream of Frank and Romi locking lips, stripping off blazers, T-shirts, expensive Chanel suits, and doing it doggy style on the break room floor with the women from Accounting cheering them on. I wake drenched with sweat, panting as if I've run three miles.

"What's wrong?" Eric asks, rolling over. He cradles me against him although I should get up and change out of my damp clothes.

"I had a bad dream," I whisper.

"More like a nightmare." He strokes hair off my forehead and kisses me. "You kept screaming, 'Don't do it, Frank,' and batting me with your arm when I tried to hold you." He pauses. "Who's Frank?"

"My boss," I say.

"What was he doing? Raping you?"

"No, no, no," I say, pulling away. "It was nothing like that."

Eric folds his arms over his chest and sulks. "Do I need to show up at work and take you out to lunch? I can wear my wife beater T-shirt and flex my muscles for the man, if you want."

"No, no, no," I say, turning back to him. "There's no need to do that."

Eric sniffs. "I wish we could afford to have you stay at home."

"It's not that bad," I assure him. "I just got promoted with a big raise and I am actually doing important work."

"For that damn bastard," Eric says.

I wince.

Eric opens his arms and pulls me close and whispers through the tangle of my hair. "Listen, I have an appointment with Black Magic on Thursday. If I can get them to agree to test my product, I can get the legal work squared away. Once the money rolls in, you can quit. Okay?"

I nod, not trusting my voice. I try to hold Eric back, but my body is tense. Some part of me does not want to give up now, not when I've come so far, so fast.

Chapter 17

The next day, Eric calls me at work. "I have good news," he says. "Katy says the Harvest Fair committee will accept your entry, as long as you have a total of three paintings with the same theme by Friday."

Luckily, Frank is out to lunch. I'm trying to package the documents needed for Damon to scan into PDF files for the board meeting next Monday. My hands drop a stack of papers on the floor. I stoop to gather them up. "But I have only one painting," I hiss.

"No problem," Eric says. "I'll take care of everything so you can paint tonight."

Tonight our church is sponsoring a family event to teach the children how to pray the rosary. Since we've already taught the rosary to Zenith, I guess it would be all right if I didn't go.

"But what will I paint? And what type of theme do they want?"

"I don't know," Eric says. "You're the artist, not me. Sorry, but I've got to go. I've got another call on the line."

It takes a few minutes after the phone call is over before it registers. Eric said I am an artist. Not an aspiring artist. But an artist. A warm feeling suffuses my body. I kick off my heels and curl my toes in satisfaction.

That night, Eric leaves leftovers in the refrigerator and a sticky note on the kitchen table. "PLEASE PAINT" is written in bold block letters.

Out of Balance

I heat up the leftover lasagna and set up my easel and paints. Only I can't find my palate knife. I check all the pockets in the rolling suitcase I use to store my supplies, but I find only the crappy plastic palate knives I used to teach the art docent class at Zenith's school last year. My very expensive palate knife is missing.

Fifteen minutes later, I decide I can't wait any longer. The art store is closed and Eric is expecting to come home to a masterpiece. I squeeze out a variety of blues and smear them around with a plastic palate knife.

All afternoon, between meetings and memos, I thought about what I was going to paint. I decided on a theme—palate knife paintings in primary colors—and I have a subject matter for the second painting in mind. When Frank called me into his office to take notes on some restructuring ideas he had for the bank, I made a comment about the pan pipe music he was playing from his computer. "I'm sick of this crap," he said. "But my wife says listening to world music will broaden my horizons and get me to see the world differently for the sake of the baby."

I turn the canvas upside down and begin to paint a portrait of Frank trapped in his office, listening to pan pipes and Baby Mozart, while the world of rock and roll beckons just outside his closed door.

The lasagna in the microwave is cold when I finally sit down to eat. But my second painting is finished. It is a bold statement to the feelings inspired by music. The soft lullabies compete with the hard rock. The man sits at his desk trapped between two worlds, not knowing how to get out. I am especially pleased with the man's double expression of loathing and inspiration. I hope the message is clear, although the painting is partially abstract.

The lock turns in the front door. Zenith bounds up to me and kisses my cheek. "Look what I got," she says, holding up a pearly pink rosary.

"Cool, did you get one for me, too?"

"No, but Daddy got one."

Eric shuts the front door and bends to kiss me. He stops and stares at the painting I just completed. His jaw twitches and his fist uncurls. Rosary beads clack against the table. He points an accusing finger at the painting. "That's him."

"Who?"

"Your boss. What's-his-face."

How does Eric know I painted Frank? Is he psychic? "It's a painting about music," I say. "Isn't that right, Zenith?"

My daughter glances from me to her father and back again. "Don't get me involved in your fight," she says. "I'm going to bed."

Alone, Eric and I stare at each other. I nibble on my nails that are still flecked with blue paint. Eric turns to study the painting closer. His frown softens.

"What do you think?" I ask.

He sighs. "Why are you obsessed with him? What does he have that I don't have?"

"You sound like a jealous husband."

"I'm not jealous. You're obsessed. My wife is obsessed with her boss. Shouldn't I be concerned?"

"Not anymore concerned than I should be about my husband who is obsessed with some computer product he developed."

"That's work," he says.

"Then why aren't you getting paid?"

"Because no one takes my product seriously, that's why."

"Well, no one takes me seriously at work either. Except Frank."

Eric balls his hands into fists. "Why does he count and I don't count?"

I glower at him. "You're not part of my work."

"Yes, I am. Your life is your work. Not some job you have to pay the bills." He paces back and forth across the linoleum with his hands on his hips, breathing in and out, in and out. His eyes are wide and full of fury. Maybe he'll decide this conversation is too much for him to handle and he'll disappear next door to work out with Brody until late into the night.

But Eric does not move more than a few feet back and forth across the kitchen. When he finally stops, he stands before my painting with tears in his eyes. "You don't understand me the way

I understand you," he says. "I know your painting is important to you. That's why I make time for you to do it. But you don't respect my time and my talent. And you don't trust me. That's why you keep trying to break into my profile to see what I'm up to. Because you assume it can't be anything good and productive. You think I'm all about joking around and having a good time, but I'm not. There's a serious side to me, too, and you're too obsessed with your damn boss to see it." He slowly turns toward me. His jaw quivers. "What happened to the woman I married?"

"She's right here," I say.

He slowly shakes his head from side to side. "No, she's not. She's missing." He points to the painting. "This is all I have left of her."

Chapter 18

The next day I call Vi during my morning break. I am outside in the drizzling rain under the awning with the cell phone plastered against my ear. "Pick up, pick up," I chant.

Finally, she answers.

"Thank God, you're there," I say. Then trying to mask my desperation, I begin with, "How was your date with the doctor?"

But Vi knows me too well. "What's wrong?" she asks.

I pause, not knowing how much to reveal. "Eric and I had a fight. I don't know what to do. He thinks I'm obsessed with my boss."

"Well, I don't know about that. But your boss does seem very interested in you."

"Why does everyone think Frank is out to screw me?"

"Because maybe he is."

"And maybe he's not," I say. Why did I call Vi? She's just going to side with Eric. "I'm sorry I called. I have to get back to work."

"Don't you want to hear about my date?" Vi asks.

"Of course," I say, although my interest has waned a bit.

"It was absolutely wonderful. He's so romantic. He brought candles and music and wine," she says in a sing-song voice. "I'm going to spend a few days with him next month when I'm in L.A. for a conference. Bob will have Mindi the whole week, and I'll take her during winter break. It will be absolutely wonderful."

I listen to the wistfulness in her voice and remember what Eric said last night. "Vi, can I ask you a question?"

"Of course, you can ask me anything. Whether or not I choose to answer is another matter."

I flash a half-smile. "Okay." I take a deep breath. "Have I changed a lot since you met me?"

The silence answers for her.

"Okay, what's different?" I ask.

"I'm sorry I wasn't paying attention," she says. "My boyfriend just sent me an e-mail and I was busy reading that. What did you ask?"

That's so unlike Vi to not pay attention. But I guess that's what new love will do. Mess with your mind. Make you forget important things. Like paying attention to your best friend when she's talking. "How am I different than when we first met?"

"Oh, I don't know," she says. "Though lately, you have been a little preoccupied with work."

Work. That's it, isn't it? Everything stems from the fact that I've gone back to work. Well, what else was I supposed to do? File bankruptcy?

"Fine, at least I'm not obsessed with my boss," I say.

"Oh, no, he's just obsessed with you," Vi says.

Frank is *not* obsessed with me. That's impossible. He's too busy trying to please his pregnant wife to be concerned about anything else—even World Bank.

In fact, Frank is not at work today. He and his wife have an appointment with the midwife at the spiritual birth clinic in the morning and an ultrasound at the hospital in the afternoon. In between, they are going to lunch at Organic Bistro and afterward they are going to the symphony. I won't see Frank till Thursday, when I present him with the final PowerPoint presentation Damon has helped me prepare for Monday's board meeting.

Although I don't particularly care for Damon's attitude, his work ethic is impeccable. He arrives early and stays late, making sure the entire computer network is running smoothly, from deposits to loan operations to online banking. The few times I've approached him with technology questions, he has responded with his usual you-don't-need-to-know-so-don't-ask attitude. But we're just finishing up with our joint project, and I'm dying to get inside Damon's head to see if I can figure out something about Eric.

"Do you toy with computers at home?" I ask.

Damon leans over and taps on my keyboard to pull up the presentation. "It should go smoothly without the board members having to touch their laptops at all," he explains. He glances at me sideways. "Why do you want to know what I do at home?"

I sigh. "My husband's an unemployed computer guru who can't seem to stop messing with the machine day and night. I just wanted to know if it's normal."

Damon shrugs. "How would I know? This is just my day job. At night, I act at the Vine Valley Theater. My latest role is Julius Caesar."

Oh, well. I guess that doesn't help me understand my husband any better.

"But my sister can't stop toying with her computer. She's always blogging about sewing. She posts progress pictures and solicits advertisers and collects a small income from it. Last year, she went on a one week vacation to Bermuda with her proceeds. This year, I think she's saving for the down payment on a new car."

That doesn't sound like Eric, either. He doesn't care whether or not he gets paid. He just works on his computer as if his life depended on it.

Maybe my husband is right. I don't understand him.

At noon, Romi comes by my desk and asks for some help. She slaps some wire transfers on my desk and points to the totals. "We're short staffed and I need someone with a keen eye to catch any errors in the general ledger," she says.

She looks more frazzled than she did the other day when she was intent on confessing her secret life. "You aren't my boss," I say. "You'll have to clear it first with Frank."

Romi's manicured nails tap the desk. "I've already called his cell and he said as long as you're done prepping for the board meeting, you can attend to other matters."

Who does she think she is, keeping her lover's cell number after 10 years? If I was Frank, I would have changed my number.

"Sure, fine," I say. "I'll look them over."

Once she is gone, Jim comes by. He stares at my chest and talks down at me. "I have some BSA reports that need to be filed," he says. "I called Frank and he said to give them to you."

"Why does everyone seem to have Frank's cell number?" I ask.

"Management has everyone else's phone numbers," Jim explains. "We sometimes get calls at home, if it's an emergency."

Really? Is this what I have to look forward to once I earn a room with a view?

I toss the Bank Security Act reports into my basket and sigh. Somehow I thought I would be working less by working for only one person. Never could I have imagined I would be working so much more.

I turn the key in the front door and it springs open. A scary clown with flaming green hair, a tongue as long as a whip, and blood-drenched fangs leaps at me. "Eek!" I lunge backward and the heel of my right shoe snaps off. I tumble into the grass.

The clown towers above me and chortles. "Heh, heh, heh, heh!"

The ladybug Zenith darts out of the house. "Mommy, are you all right?" She flutters beside me with her gauzy wings and black spotted red leotard and tights. Her antennae headband bobs on her head as she bends to help me up. "You broke your shoe!"

I rub my foot, thankful I did not twist my ankle. "I'll be all right. Just get that clown away from me!"

Zenith stands up and places her hands on her hips. "Daddy, go inside and change," she says. "You scared Mommy so well, she hurt herself."

Eric removes the clown mask and continues laughing. His eyes sparkle devilishly.

The muscles in my body, tense from the pressures at work, slowly relax with laughter. I playfully punch Eric's arm. "You little bugger," I say.

"You have to admit, it's pretty funny!" Eric puts the mask back on and thrusts his face toward me.

I shriek like a woman in a bad horror movie.

Zenith bats him away. "Leave her alone," she says. "And take that mask off." She stoops beside me. Her voice is grave. "Mommy, are you going to be all right? Should we call the doctor?"

I grab my stomach and laugh until tears stream down my cheeks. "No, honey, I'm fine." I glance up at the clown. "That's a great costume."

"Really?" Eric removes the mask. "You like it?"

"I don't *like* it. But I think it will scare everyone in the neighborhood."

Eric flashes a smile. "That's my intention. To be the evil clown terrorizing children and ravishing beautiful women." He bends down and nuzzles my neck with the stubble on his chin. I burst into a fit of giggles, curling up on the lawn. Zenith tries to pull her father off of me, but Eric turns around and tickles her until she tumbles down beside me, and we all three roll around on the grass.

Chapter 19

That night, after dinner, Eric suggests I start my final painting for the Harvest Fair exhibit. "You have only tonight and tomorrow night," he reminds me. "I'm taking everything down Friday morning."

But I don't want to paint, especially after last night. I don't want Eric accusing me of being inspired by my boss.

"Why don't I help you prep for your meeting with Black Magic tomorrow?" I have already cleared the dishes and wiped the table and swept the floor while Zenith takes her bath.

Eric finishes loading the dishwasher. He stands up, eyeing me closely. "You really want to help me?" he asks.

I nod. "Can't I be the supportive wife? Or has the role gone to someone else?"

Eric purses his lips. "You might have to fight Lori. She keeps calling and texting about that damn Halloween party, even though I have everything under control."

His phone beeps as if to emphasis his point.

He glances at the screen and frowns. "You're supposed to pray for your enemies. I pray every night she goes into labor early. I pray it lasts 72 hours and the hospital asks her to stay another 24 hours after that. And if God refuses to answer my prayers, I just might have to change my number."

"She's that bad?" I ask.

Eric shakes the phone in his fist. "Control freak central," he says. "Remind me never to accept another classroom position from anyone, regardless of the circumstance."

"Are you sure?" I ask, knowing how much of a sucker Eric is when it comes to helping the kids.

"Absolutely." He turns the phone off and shoves it into his front pocket and grabs me by the waist and pulls me close for a long, deep kiss.

We say our evening prayers as a family in Zenith's room. After Eric kisses Zenith goodnight, she grabs my hand and pulls me down onto the edge of her mattress. Her eyes are wide and sad. "I miss you, Mommy."

"I'm right here," I say, stroking her hair off her forehead. She smells of candy shampoo and bubble gum toothpaste.

She thrusts her lower lip in a pout. "I don't get to see you anymore"

"Well, you see me every night and every weekend."

"I mean alone," she says. "We never go out to ice cream alone, or shopping alone, or anything alone anymore. There's always Daddy or Mindi with us."

I think about it for a while. She's right. Since I've been working, I have not had the chance to spend time alone with her like I used to. "Tell me what you would like to do and we'll do it together. Just the two of us."

A tiny crease forms between her eyebrows as she thinks. "I know," she says, "we'll paint our nails like ladybugs."

My lower back tightens. I don't believe the dress code allows for red nails with black polka dots.

"Maybe after the board meeting on Monday," I tell her, "right before Halloween."

"Perfect!" She sits up and throws her arms around my neck. "I love you, Mommy. You're the best mommy in the whole world."

I sit on the sofa in the living room while Eric explains his project to me. His hands move quickly and his eyes flash with excitement as he talks about IP addresses, metasploits, and firewalls. I tuck my legs under my hips and listen. The more Eric talks, the more I am propelled back to our dating days when Eric shared an apartment with a gaming programmer we nicknamed Sully Rat because the guy's room looked like a mouse trap and he always moped about whenever he did not have a joy stick in his hands. Eric interned at the same company as a Junior Quality Assurance Tester, but I knew he aspired to greater things than locating the programming bugs that existed in the race to save the universe of Star Games. Whenever Eric got discouraged because one of his suggestions was dismissed at work, I always encouraged him by saying, "I believe in you. And someday, someone else will, too."

Eric finishes talking. He waits a moment for the information to sink in before he asks, "What do you think?"

Although Eric tried to use lay terms to explain complex concepts, I still do not grasp everything he said. But I do think I have an idea of what he has been working on. "You've created the ultimate child proof lock to keep people out," I say, smiling.

Eric laughs. "I wouldn't call it that exactly, but I guess from your point-of-view as a parent, it is kind of like that. Only I'm dealing with network security. If government agencies started using this product, we would have a lot fewer problems than we currently do." He brings up an article in *Tech Journal* about hackers who broke into the web portals of sites operated from the office of the Prime Minister of Bangladesh and threatened to start a Cyber War.

Eric swivels in the office chair and pivots forward, clasping his hands between his knees. His steady gaze is far from joking. "The need for cybersecurity is global. No one knows how to handle things effectively, but I'm hoping my product might pave the way to greater things."

No wonder Eric has been so secretive. He has been working on something that has the potential to change the world.

I reach over and place my hand on his knee. "This is your dream," I say, "and you're so close to having it come true. I hope God is right by telling you to contact Black Magic."

"God is always right," Eric says. "It's whether or not we listen that's the problem."

I glance away, hoping Eric is not referring to me and my poor listening skills.

He squeezes my hand. "Thanks for listening."

Our eyes meet. All the fights and disagreements dissolve in the warmth of understanding. Eric pulls me into his lap and starts kissing me. I return his kisses eagerly, my hands caressing his smooth scalp, his hands traveling down my back.

Mmm. This must be what God meant when He said, "And the two shall become one."

Chapter 20

The next day, Frank slaps a drum roll on my desk and says, "Come into my office. I have a surprise for you."

I glance nervously around, wondering what the surprise could be. Surely, it's confidential if he's asked me to step inside his office.

Frank places the aviator sunglasses on the top of his head and takes off his gray blazer. His biceps flex against his short-sleeved T-shirt and I glance away. I haven't stared at a guy since last summer at the beach when the teenage lifeguard leapt into the ocean to save a small boy from drowning. At the time, I had been mesmerized by the lifeguard's powerful legs. But this is my boss. I should not be staring. If I stare at Frank's arms, I am as guilty as Jim for ogling my breasts.

"I know I have it somewhere." Frank rifles through the pockets of his blazer. His forearms flex as he moves. I know shouldn't be staring at Frank's muscles, especially since I have a hunk of a husband at home, but Frank isn't built like Eric. Eric's muscles are big, like inflated balloons. Frank's muscles are small and sinewy, like tightly knotted rope. Maybe if I stop standing around I won't be tempted to gawk like a silly school girl. Quickly, I walk around the desk to help him, but Frank waves me away.

"Found it!" He withdraws a tiny box and slides it across the desk.

I stare at the box, afraid to touch it.

"Go ahead, open it." He sits down and turns on some music. ZZ Top sings, "Cheap Sunglasses."

I sink into the adjacent chair and grab the box off the desk. Tentatively, I tear off the glossy turquoise blue paper and lift the lid.

It's a necklace. I stare at it closer. What's this? The words, "Bank Better," are engraved across the center of the quarter-sized medallion. It's a Vine Valley Bank necklace.

"I thought it might make you feel more comfortable than that button you have to wear," Frank says. "Try it on."

I place the sterling silver necklace around my neck. The medallion rests against the hollow of my throat. It feels cool against my skin.

"It suits you," Frank says, studying me. "It sparkles just like your eyes whenever I ask you to take on a challenge."

I glance down at the pendant, then up at Frank. He flashes that crooked grin. I don't know what to say or do.

"Do you like it?" Frank asks.

I would have preferred a bonus or new pair of shoes, but I don't tell him that. "Yes, I do. Thank you."

"Don't thank me," Frank says. "Thank the bank." He turns back to his desk and sits down to check his e-mails. "Give your old button to Jim. He'll give it to the new teller who starts tomorrow. Is my ten o'clock meeting still on?" he asks.

"Umm. Yes. Of course." But I really don't remember. I'm too busy staring at the medallion swinging above my breasts.

When I come home that night, Eric and Zenith sit at the kitchen table carving their pumpkins into jack o' lanterns. Stringy gobs of pumpkin guts overflow from a plastic bowl in the center of the table. Pumpkin seeds roast in the oven. A pot of stew simmers on the stove. The house smells of beef and potatoes, carrots and corn.

"Did you guys eat already?" I ask.

They absently nod and continue working on carving faces with their knives.

"How was the meeting with Black Magic?" I ask.

Eric glances up, squints at my chest, and frowns. "Where did you get that necklace?"

I glance down and twirl the pendant. It flashes like a tiny mirror. "Work. It has our motto engraved on it."

Eric stands up and crosses over to me. He wipes his hands on a towel and examines the medallion. "What's this?" he asks, turning the pendant around. "Why does it say, 'Babe,' on the back?"

My shoulders stiffen. "It says 'Babe'?" I didn't bother turning the medallion around. I just assumed it was blank on the back.

Eric shakes his head. "What was wrong with the button you used to wear?"

I remove the necklace and turn the pendant around. It does say "Babe."

"It must be a mistake," I say. "Frank must have told the jeweler, 'I want it to read, "Bank Better," babe,' and she thought 'babe' was part of the inscription, but he was addressing her the way he addresses all women."

Zenith glances up. "He should take it back and ask the jeweler to fix it."

I tuck the necklace in my pant's pocket and walk toward the refrigerator. "It doesn't matter. I want to hear about your meeting with Black Magic. That's more important."

Eric follows me. "I think you're either incredibly naïve, or incredibly in denial." His breath is dangerously warm against my neck. "Your boss has the hots for you and you probably have the hots for him, too. That's why you keep staying later and later at work. We tried waiting to eat dinner with you, but we were so hungry by seven o' clock, that we decided to go ahead and have a meal without you." He lowers his voice. "I never came home after dinner when I was working full-time. And my job was full of emergencies."

I shut the refrigerator door and spin around. "You have nothing to worry about. Frank left early to be with his wife. I was working late with the Controller, Romi. She's been giving me work to do and I don't have time during my normal hours to do it." I sigh. "It's going to be busy next week since it's month end and the board meeting, and if that means I have to stay late, so be it. I'm getting paid for it now. I'm on a salary."

Zenith wedges between us and lifts her hands like a referee. "Don't fight," she says. "I hate it when you fight."

Eric and I both gaze down at our daughter with her shoulder-length brown hair pulled away from her pale face with a headband. Her wide brown eyes shine with fear and sadness. I stroke the back of her head and try to reassure her. "We're just talking, sweetheart."

"No, you're fighting. You're always fighting." Her lower lip quivers. "I wish you'd stop working, so everyone can be happy again."

"But, sweetheart, who will pay the bills?"

"We can move in with Ms. Patel and Mindi. They have enough room. Then we can all get along again."

She's serious.

Eric grabs her by the shoulders and steers her back toward the kitchen table. "No one is moving anywhere. This is our home. Daddy and Mommy are going to take a time out and talk again later."

Zenith narrows her eyes. "No more fighting, okay?"

Eric nods.

I scoop a bowl full of stew and grab a fork and head into the living room. I turn on the TV and surf through the channels, looking for something to distract me, but all I can think about is the terrified look in our daughter's eyes.

After Zenith is asleep, Eric retreats to the computer in the living room and I retreat to my easel in the kitchen. I open and close cupboards and search through drawers as quietly as possible. My palate knife rests next to the butter knives in the silverware drawer.

I wonder how it ended up among the forks, knives, and spoons, but resist asking Eric, although he probably knows. In fact, he might have placed it there. Yep, that's Eric, Mr. Efficient, reorganizing my entire house, so I can no longer find anything.

My two other paintings rest against the far wall in the kitchen. I gaze at them, trying to find inspiration to paint a third to complete the series. The swirling yellows of *End of the World* contrast with the cool blues of *Life in Music*. A pain lodges in the center of my chest.

Out of Balance

Eric wants to be my inspiration, but all I feel is rage. . .like a "Rat in a Cage." I heard the song booming from Frank's speakers this afternoon immediately after one of his crappy conference calls. I had been typing yet another memo, when the fierceness of the song hit me. He's angry. At what, I don't know. But I'm angry and I know exactly who I'm angry with. It's Eric, my perfect stay-at-home, fit and healthy, active father, and stiflingly loving husband.

With the flourish of a swordsman, I brandish the palate knife, mixing the colors into half-blended swirls. The song, "Rat in a Cage," keeps playing over and over in my mind. I slather paint onto one side of the knife and smear it across the canvas in furious strokes. An hour later, an abstract portrait of a woman trapped inside of a heart stares back at me. She is a woman swallowed by her feelings with no way out.

In the living room, Eric curses. I wipe my hands on a rag and peek around the corner. Eric slouches in front of the monitor, looking absolutely defeated. My heart contracts with pity and remorse. My arms hang limply at my sides. The anger I once felt has been drained and replaced by compassion for the man I love. I tiptoe into the living room and perch on the edge of the sofa next to Eric. He does not move. Regret darts through me. Why didn't I call before staying late at work? I could have sent a text or an e-mail to let him know what was going on. But I took him for granted. I assumed things would be all right at home, because Eric is so good at taking care of things.

I stare at the floor and wonder why I always upset the one man I want to please the most. Hallmark needs to print a card that says, "I'm sorry I keep messing up. I seem to be stuck on repeat. Please accept my apologies again and again." The card should record your voice and include a button you can push whenever you want the recipient to hear how sorry you are again. It would be so much easier than having to apologize in person. I could stick it on Eric's windshield before leaving for work and forget about it.

Eric shifts in his chair. "I thought you were painting," he says. "I'm done. Want to see it? You inspired me."

Eric jerks his head up. Our gaze meets briefly, then flickers away. An awkward silence beats between us like the refrain of a love-gone-wrong song.

"What are you working on?" I tentatively ask.

Eric sighs. His shoulders hunch forward, like he wants to curl up into a ball and roll away. It's really hard to disappear when you're over six feet and two hundred and thirty pounds of rock solid flesh. He runs his hand over his chin and glances back at the monitor as if the screen might have changed. "I was just chatting with a representative of Black Magic. They don't think they need my product. The guy said it is redundant."

"Redundant? How can it be redundant?" A new flash of fury takes root, but this time I am angry on behalf of Eric. "If it was redundant, then everyone would be so well protected, no one would worry about a cyberattack." I pause. "PG&E would have not been affected by your little program and the lights of the city would have never gone out. But that didn't happen, because PG&E did not have your product. No one has your product. And everyone needs it." My voice has risen to a high pitch, and Eric shushes me, reminding me that our daughter is sleeping down the hall.

But I can't quiet the seething anger I feel. "I thought God was never wrong," I whisper. "He told you to contact Black Magic. Why aren't they listening to you?"

Eric shakes his head. "I don't know, Bev. God works in mysterious ways."

"I'm glad you have more faith than I do." I stand up to return to the kitchen to clean up my mess.

"Bev?" Eric's voice sounds soft, almost pleading. I pivot toward him. He stares at me and I can't read his expression. It's something I have never seen before.

"Thanks for understanding me," Eric says. "I appreciate it."

My eyes are blurry and my throat feels like cotton wool. "No problem," I say. "You do the same for me." Okay, there's something else, something I need to tell him no matter how difficult it is. "I'm sorry. I should have called this afternoon to let you know I would be working late. I'm sorry I've been messing up so much lately. Please forgive me. I can't promise it won't happen again, because it seems like it takes me longer to learn things than everyone else, but I never do things to intentionally hurt you. I love you. You're everything to me."

Eric stares at me for a long time. My legs feel weak. I want to sink down on the floor and cry, but I remain standing as tall and immovable as a statue. Finally, Eric says, "I forgive you. And I'm sorry for being so mistrusting of your boss. It's not that I think you're unfaithful. It's that I don't trust other people around you. There's something hypnotic about your presence. You're smart and beautiful and talented, and sometimes I wonder why you stay with me, because I have nothing to offer you. No money, no prestige, no fancy jewelry."

"That's not true. You have yourself. You make me laugh. You love our daughter. You take care of everything while I'm away, and I know I could never pay you for everything you do at home. It costs more than what I make. And you love me. You really, truly love me more than anyone's ever loved me, or ever will love me." I rush over to him and kneel down beside him and bury my head against his knees. He strokes my hair and lifts my chin until our gazes meet, our eyes both moist with tears.

Chapter 21

The next morning, my car won't start. It's not the battery and it's not the starter. It's something with the transmission, according to Brody's dad who works as a mechanic at Auto Express. I hurry up and change into slacks and grab my backpack with my lunch and purse, and head out on my bike for work, leaving Eric with Brody's dad in our driveway.

I arrive at work ten minutes late. Jim hunches forward at the desk and gives me a once over as I pass. I stroll past Romi's office without bothering to say hello and duck into the bathroom to freshen up a bit. I nervously sit down at my desk and buzz Frank's office, but there is no answer. I take a deep breath and start my computer.

Five minutes later, Frank strolls down the hallway whistling, "Man on a Mission." He stops at my desk and asks, "Where's your necklace?"

Oh, shit.

Sorry, God, for swearing.

I touch the base of my neck and realize I left it at home tucked at the bottom of my underwear drawer. "I forgot it," I say.

"Well, go home and get it," Frank says. "It's part of the dress code." His mouth twitches like he's about to say something he might regret. Maybe he's thinking of firing me, like he fired the teller who showed up without her name badge last week.

It's only eight-fifteen and I'm already tired. Maybe I could go around the office and ask if someone has an extra button I can borrow. Then I won't have to go home. Yes, that's what I'll do.

I pick up the phone and dial Jim. "Um, hello, Jim, I was wondering if you have an extra Vine Valley Bank button I can borrow for the day."

Jim harrumphs. I can hear the click of drawers opening and closing. "Sorry," he says. "I'm all out. I can place an order for next week. How many do you need?"

Oh, shit.

Sorry, God, for swearing.

"Never mind," I say. "I need one sooner."

I pick up the phone and dial Romi. The phone rings and rings. I hang up and decide to walk around and ask whoever I can find. The girls in Accounting hush when I approach.

"Does anyone have an extra Vine Valley Bank button I can borrow?"

They gawk at me like I've just asked if I can borrow an arm or a leg.

"I just need it for today," I explain, "to comply with the dress code."

They glance at each other and begin to twitter with half-suppressed laughter.

I flush with anger. "You know, if any one of you ever needed help, I would be more than willing to extend it. I don't know why you have to be mean to me. I'm not different than any one of you."

"Oh, right," Tina says. She props up her breasts with her hands. "We're just the same."

"Want to see my sketchbook?" Lorraine titters. "I do paint-by-numbers."

Kim twirls her hair and tucks it behind her ear. "Umm, yes, Frank, I'll do whatever you say, Frank."

They're mocking me. Every single one of them.

I place my hands on my hips. "It's women like you who caused Van Gogh to cut his ear off."

I turn on my heels and stalk down the hall to Romi's office and knock on the door. Romi glances up from her Excel spreadsheet and beckons for me to enter. I step inside and shut the door. Although I don't know what to think of her after she confessed her ancient affair with Frank, I have been helping her balance a few of the general ledgers for the end of the month board report without compensation. She owes me.

"Have a seat," Romi says.

"I don't have time," I say. "I'm here to ask a tiny favor. May I borrow your Vine Valley Bank button?"

She glances down at her lapel. "Actually, it's part of the dress code. Don't you have one?"

"I did," I say. "But Frank gave me a necklace instead. And it's at home. I don't have a car today. I need a ride. It should only take a few minutes."

Romi frowns. "How did you get to work?"

"I biked," I say.

Romi leans back and crosses her legs. "I would like to help, but I have a meeting with the Chief Financial Officer at World Bank at eight-thirty. We're finalizing the figures."

I nod. Everything revolves around World Bank these days. "Okay, I'll bike home."

"Sorry," Romi says.

I try calling Eric at home, but there is no answer. He's probably with Zenith at school. Maybe I can reach him before he heads over to the fairgrounds to deliver my paintings for the art exhibit. I dial his cell, but the call rolls over to his voice mail greeting. His mail box is full, so I can't leave a message. Ugh! I send a text and hope he does not ignore it.

I wait until eight-thirty. I can't afford to waste any more time. I grab my backpack, change into my tennis shoes, strap my helmet under my chin, and stalk out of the bank into the overcast morning.

My car is not in the driveway when I arrive. I step into the empty house and walk to my bedroom and remove the necklace from my underwear drawer. The chain unwinds and the medallion glints like a coin in the sunlight. I place the pendant around my neck. It feels heavy and unwanted, like the proverbial ball and chain everyone talks about when they get married. But I am not married to the bank. I just work there, but the burden seems greater than it should.

The phone rings. I pad down the hallway and listen for the answering machine to pick up.

"Eric, it's Lori. I've been trying to call you on your cell, but the mail box is full. I wanted to know why you haven't contacted the caterers I recommended and why you insist on hosting this party yourself. I don't remember you telling me you're a professional chef, and I'm calling to remind you that last year it took three professionals to serve the food in addition to all the parents who came to help. I really think you should reconsider and hire some help. Unless you're having your own home staff assist you. In that case, I'd like to meet them this weekend and sample the food they're planning on serving before the Halloween party next Wednesday. You have my number. Call me." The answering machine clicks off.

That bitch, I think. She has a lot of gumption to call and leave that message on our home phone. What if Zenith played it back? What would she think?

No wonder Eric feels bad. The mommies are constantly badgering him about things that cost money and they do not appreciate the amount of time he has devoted to this ridiculously overrated classroom party.

The doorbell rings. I go to answer it. The UPS man stands outside the front door holding a huge package. He sets it inside the house and leaves as soon as I sign his electronic note pad. After he is gone, I read the return address. Party Central. It must be the second shipment of party supplies Eric ordered. I wonder how much money the school has donated for the party and how much has ended up on our personal credit card.

But I have no time to worry about it. Clouds have gathered in the sky. I need to bike back to work before it starts to rain.

When I return to the bank, Frank is meeting with Romi and the Chief Financial Officer of World Bank in the conference room. I sit down at my desk and rifle through my in-basket before deciding to type Frank an e-mail requesting time off to attend Zenith's classroom party next week. I do not want to miss Eric's debut as the room parent. More importantly, I want to be there to help deflect some of the criticism he will most likely receive from some of the richer, snootier mommies.

I reply to all the e-mails and answer three phone calls from the press inquiring about our sudden interest in World Bank. Each time I say, "No comment." I do not know who told what to the media, but I know enough not to answer their questions.

An hour later, Frank swaggers down the hall and slaps a drum roll on the edge of my desk. "How's it going, babe?" He surveys my body from the waist up. "Glad to see you're wearing your necklace."

I flash a quick smile and hand him the mail, sorted by priority. "I made it back before it rained," I say. "That's the only thing I was worried about."

He frowns. "Why do you care about the rain?"

"I biked to work today."

"Oh, really? My wife would love if I did that. Help sustain the earth and all that mumbo jumbo." He heads into his office and closes the door. A few minutes later, he sends me an e-mail in response to my request for time off. "We'll have to play it by ear. Still waiting for a final response from World about our offer. If we don't hear from them today, I'm canceling Monday's board meeting until further notice."

Cancel the board meeting? Until further notice? What about my PowerPoint presentation? What about all the reports I've worked on? What about all the time I've spent after hours, when I could have been home with my family being a wife and a mother?

I pick up the phone and dial the number for World Bank and ask to speak with Buddy. "He's in a meeting," his assistant says. "I don't know when it will end. Would you like to leave a message?"

Frank has already warned me against leaving messages at World Bank. "You never know if or when they'll misconstrue something, and we can't afford to make any mistakes."

I tell Buddy's receptionist I will call back. After I hang up the phone, I say a quick prayer. I need Buddy to respond to Frank's offer today. I can't afford to have this buyout drag on for another month. The stress will destroy me.

By four o'clock, I have not reached Buddy at World Bank. He is either in meetings, or screening his phone calls. I decide to leave a brief message on his voice mail in the flirtiest voice I can muster. Hopefully, it will solicit a response.

At four-thirty, I pick up a call from Eric. "Sorry it's taken me this long to get back to you," he says. "What did you call me for?"

I exhale sharply. "I needed to go home and get something. I was hoping to get a ride. That's all."

"I can pick you up from work," Eric says.

"That's all right. I can bike."

"Well, actually, I have a surprise," he says.

A slow smile spreads across my face. "Really? What is it?"

"It's a surprise," Eric says. "You're supposed to guess."

Hmm. "Is it a new car?"

He laughs. "No, but Carl's going to fix your old car at his shop and we can pay him next week when your raise kicks in."

Oh, bummer. So much for a Mercedes.

"Is it a spa getaway?"

"Close, but not quite."

Hmm. No spa? Possible getaway?

"You're taking me on a date?" It better not be at Home Depot.

"Bingo! I'll pick you up at five, okay?"

"Maybe I'll just bike to Home Depot and meet you there."

Eric laughs. "No, it's not that kind of date."

"Then what kind of date is it?"

"The kind your fairy godmother would dream up, if you had one."

Fairy godmother? Fancy dinner? Dancing? "Oo-la-la, I can hardly wait."

At four-thirty, Frank calls me into his office. I perch on the edge of the chair facing his massive desk with a notebook propped against my knee. *Please, God, let it be good news. Please, please, please,* I pray.

Frank leans back in his leather executive chair and props his feet on the desk. Baby Mozart plays through the speakers. "My wife is having a girl," he says. "We are thinking of naming her Star. What do you think?"

Star? Like I named my daughter, Zenith? "Sounds good," I say. "I'm sure she'll be happy with it."

He bobs his head in time with the sweet violins and rests his fingertips in the shape of a pyramid. "I want you to cancel the board meeting on Monday. Just attach your PowerPoint presentation to an e-mail and follow up with a phone call to all the board members. As you know, we're still finalizing things with World and we won't have an answer till after the first of the month."

Humph. This thing could drag on and on until Christmas.

"Oh, and one more thing," Frank says, lifting one finger. "I need you to come into work early on Monday to go over our strategy, in case World decides it wants to counter. I've already told them we are not negotiating, and the FDIC is prepared to take them over November 15, but I don't want them to know that's our backup plan. I want to keep them guessing."

I take a deep breath and hold it. Why should we try to strategize when the deal is pretty much done? It sounds absolutely pointless.

I slowly exhale and try to find a bit of calmness in the quagmire of emotions I'm feeling. I really don't want to come into work early without a board meeting to attend. I really don't want to field phone calls from the media, deflect their questions politely, and pretend everything is fine, when it is not. World Bank's finances are all messed up from what I can see, and I really don't think buying them out will solve our problems, since we could use more cash reserves if the recession continues and businesses continue to layoff employees and cut back on expenses. I've already told Romi this and she has promised to mention it at the board meeting on Monday, but that meeting has been postponed.

"Frank, I really think we should reconsider buying out World Bank." My fingers twirl the pen in my hand. "I don't think we can afford it. I've looked at the big picture and tallied up all the little things that make up the big picture, and I think it would be best to let them go to the FDIC. We don't need to inherit their headaches. We have enough of our own."

"Really?" Frank removes his feet from his desk and sits up. "What type of headaches do we have?"

I glance down at my notes. "We have problems with the last three construction loans in our portfolio that have not moved over into non-accrual. There are no security measures to prevent identity theft. Our OFAC reports are filed away, even when we have a positive hit. And we have no standardized policies and procedures from what I can tell. And yes, I've searched the intranet and the hard copy manuals in our library."

I resist biting the end of my pen to keep myself from shaking.

Frank stares at the floor, absorbing my list of complaints. "Well, I think we can ignore the construction loans. We no longer offer the product to our borrowers, so it's a question of managing the ones we have left with updated procedures. We have IT researching security software programs to protect our database from internal and external compromises. I haven't been keeping up with the Office of Foreign Assets Control reports. I'll have to ask Tim in Compliance about that." He sighs. "I guess you could start writing a manual for the bank with our latest and greatest policies and procedures. If you don't have time during your regularly scheduled hours, I could get Damon to program your access key for longer hours. You could also work weekends."

Shit, that's not what I was hoping for. I was just trying to avoid the whole acquisition of World Bank, not create more work for myself.

"I think I can manage to squeeze it into my current workflow," I say, crossing my fingers just in case I am wrong.

Frank glances at the clock. "Oh, well, I've got to get going. My wife and I have plans tonight. We can resume discussions on Monday at seven-thirty, okay?"

Seven-thirty. Even if my car isn't fixed yet, Eric can drop me off to work on the way to Zenith's school. "Yes, that would be fine."

I stand up to leave.

"Hey, babe, thanks for the input." Frank flashes his crooked smile, and the tension in my shoulders eases just a tiny bit. "I'm glad to have you on our team."

I twirl the necklace at the base of my throat. "I'm glad to be part of the team," I say, although I don't really feel like it.

At five o'clock, Jim calls me to the front desk. Eric and Zenith stand in the lobby admiring the painting Frank bought on our trip to Spa County. "Hey, it looks just like your sketch, only in color," Eric says, hugging me.

"Mmm." I tilt my head to gaze at the painting. "I think it's better than my work."

Zenith tugs on my arm. "Mommy, we have a surprise for you."

"I know, honey." I bend down toward her. "Are you going to tell me what it is?"

She shakes her head. "You're going to have to guess."

"Hmm. Daddy said he's taking me on a date."

"Not just any date. A special date."

Eric removes two tickets from his back pocket. "We are going to the exclusive art show reception at the Harvest Fair. Courtesy of Katy."

Romi squeezes past us as she heads toward the double glass doors. A quick smile flickers across her face. "Is this your family, Bev?"

"Oh, yes," I say. "This is my husband, Eric, and my daughter, Zenith. And this is Romi, the Controller. She takes care of all the bank's finances."

Romi shakes Eric's hand. "Your wife is fabulous with numbers. I hope you didn't mind me stealing her for a few hours after work this week. She has a keen eye. I could use her full-time in my department, only Frank won't give her up." She smiles at Zenith. "Are you good at math, like your mommy?"

Zenith shrugs. "I don't know what I'm good at."

"That's fine," Romi says. "You have plenty of time to figure it out." Her cell phone rings. "Nice meeting you both. I'm sure I'll see you again." She fishes in her purse and retrieves the phone. Her voice echoes against the high ceilings, then disappears as soon as she leaves the building.

"Good with numbers, eh?" Eric studies me carefully, as if seeing me for the first time. "Ready to go?" he asks. "We'll drop Zenith off at Vi's house where we'll get changed into our evening attire."

Oo-la-la, evening attire. Sounds absolutely magical. I slip my arm into the crook of Eric's elbow. "Let's go."

Chapter 22

I feel like Cinderella with Prince Charming entering the exhibit hall. I am wearing a sapphire sheath borrowed from Katy and silver shoes that Eric grabbed from my closet. Eric sports a charcoal colored Valentino suit he rented from the Men's Warehouse. It flatters the shape of his body, highlighting all the hard work he's spent developing his muscles. I slip my hand in the crook of his elbow and squeeze the silky wool fabric. Eric cups my fingers with his hand and smiles. He bends so close I can smell his minty toothpaste. "You're the most beautiful woman in the room," he says.

That's a great compliment, because the exhibit hall is full of beautiful women in glamorous evening gowns and handsome men in expensive suits. They mill about the room sipping champagne and nibbling hors d'oeuvres. Some of them scribble notes about which paintings they are going to buy at the end of the night. It's one of the prerequisites of the exhibit—every piece of artwork is an original painting for sale. I was too flustered thinking about the possibility of anyone buying any of my paintings, so I let Eric price them for me. He showed them to Katy, who suggested selling them at $1,500 a piece. Eric said that was a little steep, so he settled on $500. When he told me, I thought the price was still a little high.

"Where are your paintings?" Eric asks.

I scan the room. There are so many paintings. Country landscapes, seascapes, mountain retreats, figure paintings, and abstracts. It takes a moment for my eyes to focus. Once they do, I quickly realize Katy was right. Fifteen hundred seems to be the going rate for most of the artwork on display. I feel a bit under priced. Oh, well, maybe that means someone will actually buy the paintings. Then I won't be an aspiring artist anymore. I'll be able to call my parents and tell them I'm a professional.

Above a crowd of onlookers, I spot my vivid abstracts. "Over on the far left wall," I say.

"Let's go." Eric tugs me closer and kisses the top of my head. "I'm so proud of you."

I feel my face flush with color.

A waiter carrying a platter of champagne flutes approaches us. "Champagne?"

"Thank you." Eric hands me a glass. "A toast. To my very talented wife."

Our glasses click. The drink fizzles against my tongue, and the bubbles seem to rise instantly to my head. This surprise is overwhelming. It surely makes up for the date at Home Depot.

I lift my glass. "Another toast. To my supportive husband who is equally talented in a different kind of art."

Eric laughs. "So, you're calling my tinkering around with the computer an art form?"

"Why not?"

"I guess the dancing clowns were a pretty cool touch," he says. He stares off as if remembering the moment he launched his spyware and virus removal program with the dancing clowns at the end. "Your parents still call me Joke'em."

For a second, I consider whether or not Eric will play a joke on me tonight. But the longer I gaze into his bright eyes, the more confident I feel he will be on his best grown up behavior.

"Hey, babe."

I stop walking. I *know* that voice. My lower back tenses.

"I didn't expect to see you here."

I glance over my shoulder. Frank stands behind me cradling a glass of scotch. He's dressed in a suit I've never seen before and his sunglasses are tucked into his breast pocket instead of perched on the top of his wavy salt and pepper hair. He winks at me. "Nice dress."

Oh, no. There is no way Eric is going to behave tonight.

My throat feels dry. I take a gulp of champagne. "Umm. Hi. What brings you here?"

"I've come to see the exhibit. My wife and I attend every year. And you?"

"Umm."

"She has three pieces on display," Eric says.

Frank's gaze soaks him in. "Who are you?"

Eric laughs. "I'm the genie in the lamp. Many rub, but rub the wrong way. Bev, on the other hand, rubbed me just right." He wraps his arm around my waist and tugs me toward him. "I gave her three wishes. The first wish was to come here tonight. The second wish—"

"Frank, this is my husband, Eric." I wiggle out of Eric's embrace and force a smile. "Eric, this is my boss, Frank."

Eric's eyes glint with mischief. "What an unexpected pleasure." Eric reaches out and shakes Frank's hand a little too hard.

Frank winces.

"I see you've come alone," Eric says.

"My wife is in the restroom," Frank explains. He flexes his fingers as if trying to get the blood to circulate again. "Pregnancy changes you. We make lots of pit stops these days."

Eric nods. "Oh, I remember those days."

Frank turns toward me. "Where are you paintings?"

I glance nervously at the wall.

"We were just going to go look at them," Eric says. "Why don't you join us?" His eyes flash with merriment.

I gaze at Frank pleadingly, hoping he can read my mind. *Please, say no. Please, please, please, say you need to stay here and wait for your wife.*

Frank takes a swig of scotch and smiles broadly. "It would be my pleasure."

The three of us stroll awkwardly toward the far left wall and scan the paintings. My three abstract paintings hang just slightly above eye level. The first painting is *Life in Music* followed by *Heart Cage* and *End of the World*. Frank slowly sips his scotch and studies my paintings thoughtfully. Eric watches Frank with intense interest.

I stand between the two men feeling oddly out of place, wishing I could duck somewhere and hide.

"I like the red painting the best," Frank says. "It seems to capture the feeling of entrapment brought out by a passionate and all consuming love."

"Yeah, well, my favorite is *End of the World*," Eric says. "It's the ultimate orgasm. See how the colors just explode."

"I love the shades of blue in the first painting," a woman says. "It's as calming as a lullaby."

I gaze at the woman. She looks strangely familiar. Her long blond waves cascade over her shoulders. She wears a floral maternity dress and Birkenstock sandals.

"This is my wife, Sandy. This is my assistant, Beverly, and her husband, Eric." He turns back toward the paintings. "These paintings are Bev's. I mentioned she was an artist, didn't I?"

"I'm sure you did, dear, but you know I never listen to anything when you talk about work." She nudges his arm playfully. "They're getting ready to seat for dinner. Want to stand in line? I'm starving."

"No, you can go ahead and save a place for me. I think I'll look around a little more, okay?"

"Sure, dear." She waves at Eric and me. "Nice meeting you both."

When she is gone, Eric says, "Maybe I should stand in line for us?"

I narrow my gaze at Eric. This is a test, isn't it? He wants to see if I will go with him, or if I will stay with Frank and visit a little bit longer. He wants to see which man I choose. Well, I'm smarter than that. I'm not going to fall for his little trap. I clutch Eric's sleeve. "I'll go with you."

Eric's eyes twinkle devilishly. "Maybe you and your boss have a little catching up to do outside of work." He smiles mischievously. "Besides, I can't make a pregnant woman stand in line all by herself. What if she goes into labor?"

This is definitely a setup. Sandy isn't that pregnant. Six, maybe seven months, tops.

I squeeze Eric's forearm and motion toward the adjacent room where dinner will be served. "We'll go together," I say, feeling determined to outsmart him.

"No, no, no," Eric insists, uncurling my fingers from his forearm. "You are the artist. You should enjoy the spotlight for a while longer."

"But—"

"Let him go," Frank says. "He'll be good company for Sandy."

I feel dejected once Eric leaves. For a moment, I wonder if I was wrong and he was not trying to set me up for a fall. Maybe he would rather stand in line with a pregnant stranger than with me. I stare at him in line with Sandy. He talks with her and the others in line with him. Every now and then, he glances over at me. I bet he's secretly spying on me, hoping I will misbehave. Oh, well, he's going to be disappointed. I step away from Frank and pretend to admire the other paintings along the wall. I hope Eric can see I am on my best behavior, even if he isn't. I can keep my focus away from my boss, even though he stands a few feet away from me, admiring my paintings.

"I didn't know you painted abstracts," Frank says. "I thought you were a more realistic artist from your sketches."

"Normally, I am. But lately I've been feeling things I cannot express and this is what came out." I motion toward the panel of paintings. My gaze stops at *Life in Music*. "I painted that one for you."

Frank nods thoughtfully and finishes his glass of scotch. "My wife noticed. She notices everything, even though she says she doesn't." He stares at the ice cubes at the bottom of his glass as if they might hold the answers he is searching for. When he looks up, our eyes meet. I swallow the last of my champagne and glance around for the waiter to get another glass.

"Are you happy, Bev?"

The question surprises me. I manage to catch the attention of a waiter and exchange my empty glass of champagne for a full one. Frank places his glass on the platter and grabs a flute of champagne. "A toast to you," he says. "I hope your paintings take Best of Show."

Our glasses click. We sip in silence. I have not answered his question.

"I take your silence as a no," Frank says.

"I am happy," I say, a little too hurriedly. "I was just taken aback by the question. No one at work asks questions like that."

"We're not at work."

I study him carefully. There are creases at the corners of his dark eyes. His jaw tenses. He lifts the glass of champagne to his mouth with increased patience. There are tiny hairs on his knuckles. His wedding ring is just a solid gold band like mine. I don't even remember noticing what his wife was wearing. Maybe they have matching sets like Eric and I. "Are you happy?" I finally ask him.

Frank flashes his crooked smile. "No, I'm not. I'm scared to death of becoming a father."

He has no problem managing billions of dollars, but he has a problem managing his fear of parenthood.

I touch his sleeve. "You'll be fine."

He gaze lingers where my fingers once were. "I don't feel fine."

"It's scary," I say, remembering those first few weeks of no sleep and constant feedings and diaper changes. "But you'll get used to it. When you look into your daughter's face, all the fear will melt away and be replaced with love. Even the frustration will dissipate. Trust me. I've done it. And I was scared, too."

"You were scared? I thought all women were natural mothers."

I laugh. "Eric is the natural parent in our house. I had to learn the hard way through on-the-job-training. It gets easier though. Just remember to be kind to yourself and lean on your spouse every now and then."

"Every now and then," he echoes.

I turn around and notice Eric pointing at the open doors. "They're going into dinner. Let's go."

"Wait."

The urgency in his voice stops me. I pause, wondering what he wants to say that has not already been said.

"Thank you, babe."

I smile tentatively. "You're welcome."

***

"So what did you two talk about?" Eric asks.

"Oh, don't you wish you'd stayed and listened," I tease.

We are sitting several tables away from Frank and Sandy. Eric said we didn't have gold tickets, just silver ones, so we have to sit farther back. I don't care. I'm just glad to be here. The auditorium style room is decorated festively with harvest green and gold streamers and clusters of balloon bouquets in similar colors. Soft golden candlelight glints from each round table. The chatter of competing conversations fills the room. The scent of rosemary and garlic and roasted chicken and buttery bread wafts through the room from a swinging door leading to the kitchen.

Eric whispers in my ear, "Did your boss say anything about the genie in the lamp, or the ultimate orgasm?"

I unfold my napkin and place it on my lap and reach for a piece of warm bread. "No, he didn't. We talked about personal things."

"Like what color is your underwear?"

I giggle. "No, silly, he's afraid of parenthood. That's all."

"Ah, the macho man can't be macho with a kid." Eric nods. "Good thing I didn't tell him I'm a stay-at-home dad. He might want to sign up and take lessons, and my schedule is booked through the end of the year."

"Ha-ha. Very funny. He happens to be genuinely concerned about it."

"That's his wife's problem, not yours." Eric sips from his glass of iced water. "I understand why you're so humorless these days. Your boss has no funny bone whatsoever. I've never seen anyone so dour. No wonder you're stressed out."

"He's not always that way," I say, thinking of the times he comes into the bank whistling a song by ZZ Top or Van Halen and slapping a drum roll on my desk.

A group of waiters winds their way around the tables setting salads before us. I pour the ranch dressing over the baby red tomatoes, cucumber slices, and butter lettuce. Through the throng of people, I can see Frank sitting next to his wife. She is talking animatedly to the person next to her. He rests his arm on the back of her chair and glances over his shoulder, as if he can feel me staring at him. I quickly turn toward Eric, hoping Frank didn't see me gazing at him. My heart patters in my chest. My hand quivers slightly as I touch Eric's arm. "How was it getting to know Sandy?"

Eric shrugs. "She's just another colorless human being intent on saving the world through organic this and that. A few times, I wanted to tell her to just stop breathing. No more carbon dioxide. That will save the planet. But I was good. You should be proud of me. I didn't upset her." He smiles as if he is pleased with himself. "Besides, I already have one crazy pregnant woman to deal with."

"How is Lori nowadays?"

"Bossy as ever," Eric says. "I've got the party covered though. I'm going to try out a few recipes this weekend and the rest is being handled by the other parents. I've got quite the setup going. Delegate, delegate, delegate."

We finish our salad just before the entrees are served. The woman beside me introduces herself as Valerie Moreno, the Museum Curator, and the man next to her as her boyfriend, Ted Nichols, the owner of the new art gallery downtown. Eric starts chatting with them about art history and economics, and my mind drifts to other things. The chicken is a little tough compared to how Eric cooks it at home. And the rice pilaf, although fragrant, is a bit chewy. But what I hate the most are the overcooked, soggy vegetables in a garlic-infused butter sauce.

I move my fork across the plate, pretending to listen to the conversation and eat. Eric's phone beeps. He glances down to check a text message. "Yes!" He pumps his fist into the air. "She's in labor! Woo-hoo! Now if it only takes her till Thursday to be released from the hospital, I'll be fine."

I calculate the math in my head. "But that's six days. No one stays six days in the hospital after giving birth, unless something goes wrong."

Eric's eyes twinkle. "No one said I was a saint."

I nudge him in the ribs. "You shouldn't wish for bad things to happen, even to bad people."

Valerie leans toward us. "Who are you talking about?"

"Some pushy broad who expects me to serve a twelve course meal on silver plates to a bunch of eight-year-olds on Halloween," Eric explains. "She's on bed rest till she gives birth. The message I just received says she's on her way to the hospital. Hopefully, that means she's in labor and she'll leave me alone for a few days."

"She left a message at the house today," I say.

Eric raises his eyebrows. "Really? How do you know?"

"I listened to it when I came home to get something for Frank. She sounded distraught that she couldn't reach you."

"That's her." He chuckles and lifts his glass of iced water. "Here's to pregnant women and Halloween parties. May they both be over with soon."

Our glasses click. I finish my second glass of champagne. Eric pours me a glass of water from the pitcher on our table. As soon as the waiters serve dessert, the Chairman of the Harvest Fair committee approaches the podium. He is a shaggy-haired, forty-something man dressed in a baggy suit. The microphone crackles. Chatter from the tables stops. Everyone focuses their attention on him as he drones on and on in a monotone voice about the history of the Harvest Fair.

Between the heads of people at our table, I glimpse Frank leaning close to his wife and whispering into her ear. They stand up and start to leave. I catch Sandy's gaze and she waves goodbye. Frank trails behind her. He stops at our table and rests his hand on my bare shoulder. A zing of electricity shoots through me. "See you early Monday morning, babe." He gives my shoulder a squeeze before letting go.

I lean back and relax once Frank has left the room. Everything feels so much lighter.

Eric reaches for my hand and whispers, "They're going to announce the winners. The grand prize is $25,000. Can you imagine what we could do with $25,000?"

My shoulders tense. I have no illusions about winning, although it would be nice to have an extra $25,000 in the bank for winning Best of Show. But that's a fantasy. I have no formal training, no gallery exhibits on my resume, no praise from art critics, and no loyal following from a group of fans. I'm just someone who paints to record the important moments of her life.

"And Best of Show goes to Marc Andre Souza for his painting, *Social Media Blizzard*."

Oh, yes, I remember that painting. It's a brilliant fusion of surrealism and technology. Pieces of a motherboard are pasted onto the canvas. Text messages scroll across profile pictures. It's all tied together with wonderfully thick brushstrokes.

"Mr. Souza is going to be our headlining artist next year," Ted says. "Do you have any gallery showings coming up?"

I shake my head. "I paint for fun. This is my first exhibit."

Eric reaches across the table and hands Ted one of my business cards from Vine Valley Bank. "She has a closet full of paintings. If you would like to see them, you can call her for an appointment."

I flush with embarrassment. "Really, Eric, that's not necessary."

Eric gazes at me meaningfully. "I'm the genie in the lamp," he says. "I'm here to grant all your wishes."

Chapter 23

I think the evening went well between the art exhibit, the dinner, and Eric meeting my boss, until Eric and I are in the car driving to pick up Zenith from Vi's townhouse.

Eric accelerates a little too fast along the freeway onramp. His hands grip the steering wheel too tightly and his voice is edged with frustration. "Why did you tell Ted you don't want to have an art exhibit?"

I shrug and turn up the heater and slip off my shoes. "I paint for fun, not money."

Eric lifts his eyebrows and moves to the fast lane. The lights from the oncoming cars in the other lane zip by like lightning bugs. "If you made money from your art, you wouldn't have to work anymore."

My shoulders tense. "You mean I wouldn't have to work for the bank anymore, which means I wouldn't have to work for Frank anymore, which is what you really mean."

"Don't assume I'm a jealous husband, because I'm not. I just don't like you selling yourself short."

"I'm not selling myself short," I say. "I'm not selling myself at all."

"That's the problem," Eric says. "You need to do something to make things happen. Otherwise, you'll just let outside influences determine your destiny."

I laugh. "You've been hanging out with Vi too much. All your psycho-babble means nothing to me. I paint because I have to.

If I painted for money, it would be a job. And it wouldn't be fun anymore."

"Can't you have fun at a job?" Eric turns off the freeway and accelerates up the hill toward Vi's townhouse.

"Jobs are for paying the bills. Hobbies are for pleasure. Some people are lucky and they can do what they love and make money at it. But the rest of us have to make sacrifices." Smoky air from cozy fireplaces blows in through the vents of the car. My throat is tight. "Let's not talk anymore. I don't want to spoil an otherwise perfect evening."

Eric swings into Vi's driveway and parks.

I open up the car door and stalk out into the clear, chilly air. It feels like the whole world has turned upside down with the empty darkness of the night sky above contrasting with the belly full of a hundred thousand tiny lights shining from the city below.

Eric stalks around the car and offers his hand. "Ready?"

I shake my head. "I never wanted to work."

Eric drops his hand to his side and his broad shoulders sag forward. He looks like a beaten dog. But I do not say anything. I just wrap my arms tighter across my body trying to warm up.

"I know," Eric says. "That's why I'm trying to help."

I sigh. "Stop trying. I'm doing what I have to do to keep our lives above water. Isn't that enough? Do I really have to gain pleasure from the sacrifice? Really, what do you want from me? Because I've already given everything I have to give."

Eric remains speechless. I walk past him up to the door and ring the bell and wait for Vi to answer. But it's Zenith. "Mommy! How was it?"

I step inside and wait for Eric. But he does not move from where he stands with his back toward the house and his hands shoved into his pockets. I can't tell if he's staring at the lights or his feet.

"Why is Daddy not coming inside?" Zenith asks.

"He needs a time out," I say, shutting the door.

Vi sits on the sofa with her laptop, typing quickly and smiling.

"What are you doing?" I ask, sitting down beside her and glancing at the screen.

She snaps the laptop closed. "Just chatting with Dr. Feel Good."

"Chatting adult talk?"

She glances anxiously away.

Okay, she's sexting with her new boyfriend while my daughter is still up. What is this world coming to?

"How was the reception?" Vi asks.

I shrug, feeling less than enthusiastic. "Eric is upset, because I turned down an offer from a gallery owner to look at my artwork."

"Why did you do that?"

I shrug. "I'm a confessional artist. I paint to record memories. I don't have a grand statement to make about the world." I sit down next to Vi. She sets the laptop on the coffee table and turns toward me with a professionally attentive expression on her face. "The guy who won Best of Show paints beyond his memories. His painting showed how technology intersects with the friendships in our lives. I just painted about my feelings. That's the difference. And I'm okay with that, but Eric's not. He wants me to make money from my art."

Vi glances around the room and frowns. "Where is Eric?"

Zenith points to the closed front door. "Mommy says he's having a time out."

Vi gazes at me meaningfully. "Do you want to go to the kitchen and have a cup of tea? Zenith can stay overnight. Bob isn't coming until noon to pick Mindi up."

I stand up. "No, thanks. I'm tired. It was a long night. I'd rather just go home and sleep."

Vi continues to stare at me like she's worried. Why can't everyone just leave me alone? I just want to be without judgment for once.

Zenith walks over to me and grabs my hand. "I'm sorry you didn't win," she says.

I squeeze her hand. "That doesn't matter. I was afraid to show my artwork to anyone other than you and Daddy. But I took a chance and let Daddy enter it into the exhibit. I'm surprised I didn't feel bad about everyone looking at my art. I'm usually self-conscious. But I wasn't tonight. And that's enough to make me happy."

By the time we step outside, Eric is back in the car with the engine running. Zenith hops into the back seat. "Love you, Daddy," she says.

He glances in the rearview mirror. "Love you, too, sweetheart."

I slide into the seat beside Eric and shut the door.

We drive home in silence.

Later that night, I wake up without Eric beside me. I pad down the hallway into the kitchen for a glass of water and notice Eric sitting in the glow of the computer's monitor in the living room. He minimizes the screen as soon as he hears my footsteps, and the room blinks from white to black.

I ignore him. How many times have I woken up in the middle of the night to find Eric sitting at the computer reading the news, or watching porn, or writing a program that will wipe out a virus or break into a network? I really don't think I can count that high. And I really don't care anymore.

I leave the kitchen with a tall glass of cold water and shuffle through the living room without saying a word.

"Are you still mad at me?" Eric asks.

I shrug and continue walking.

"Come here," he says. "I want to show you something."

What does he want to show me? How the latest study shows that the radio frequency from cell phones produces brain cancer? Or how it's normal for someone to get turned on by a video of a bunch of guys masturbating to a woman touching herself? Or how his latest software program can break into the White House and turn off the President's automatic coffee maker without anyone suspecting it was foul play?

I reluctantly shuffle over to him. Eric takes the glass out of my hand, takes a sip, and sets it on the table before tugging me into his lap. I rest my head against his chest and smell his musky sweat. His breath is slow and shallow against my quickened heartbeat. I shift my body, trying to get comfortable against the firm contours of his chiseled abs. Eric brings up the screen he had minimized and types a few keystrokes.

"Watch this," he says.

I sit up in his lap and stare at the screen. A program launches from our computer and breaks through a firewall to access Mike's computer at his law office. A clown dances across the screen, followed by two more clowns who form a circle. The three clowns hold hands and sing, "Ring around the Rosy," before exploding into a bloody mess.

"What was that about?" I ask.

Eric laughs. "I was just testing to see if this worked. I'm going to launch this program against Black Magic's network and take them down," he says. "It'll show them they need my product."

"But how will they know it was you? And how will they know you did it on purpose to show them they need to support your product?"

Eric nods toward the screen. The bloody mess from the dead clowns form the words, "You've been hacked by Joke'E.M. Prepare to negotiate or die."

My lips tighten into a straight line. I can't believe Eric thinks he can break into the ultimate hacker club's network to show them who's the boss without getting into trouble. "Won't they send someone out to take care of you? Like a mafia hit man or something?"

Eric laughs. "They don't know where I'm located. That's the beauty of my program. It's absolutely fool-proof."

I stare into his twinkling eyes and feel a stab of fear. "Why don't you just go to Silicon Valley and pitch your product to a bunch of venture capitalists?"

"Mike already tried that route," Eric says. "No one is interested in investing right now, especially in a product like mine where the need can't be shown without ruffling a few feathers."

"So, you have to go underground, or move onto something else?" I say.

"Exactly." He squeezes me tight. "Do you like it?"

I don't know what to say. Eric will launch the program whether I tell him to or not. I should be thankful he has informed me so that

I have been warned if some small blurb appears in the daily news about his latest anonymous exploit, but part of me just can't let go of the anger I feel. Maybe I should try some reverse psychology and tell Eric I agree with him wholeheartedly. Then Eric will abandon his plan to break into Black Magic's network, and I won't have to worry anymore. By that time, the purchase of World Bank should be over, and I can talk to Frank about giving Eric a business loan.

I snuggle closer to Eric. "Do you think this is the only way to get the results you seek?"

Eric rubs my back while he thinks. "I don't know if it's the only way. But it's the only way I know."

Okay. I sit up straighter to mask my doubts. Reverse psychology, here I come.

"I guess it's worth a try." I touch his cheek and he smiles against my hand. It's working. He believes me. The anger I feel slowly melts away. It is replaced by an enduring hope that everything will turn out all right.

Eric chuckles. "Oh, yeah, honey. It's more than worth a try. It *will* get the job done. They'll definitely notice they need my product, and then I can negotiate for what I want on my terms."

Chapter 24

On Saturday afternoon, we try out some of the recipes Eric has selected for the Halloween party. Zenith wants to make the kitty litter cake and Eric wants to try the gelatin brain mold he bought online. I think a plateful of chocolate-covered cherry mice might be nice. The roasted ghoul tongues (chicken slices), candied bugs and slugs (fruit and nut mix), mummy dogs (hot dogs wrapped in croissants), and spooky Halloween pizza (with olives and sausages strategically placed to look like eye of newt and gopher nuts) are easy, according to Eric, and don't need a test run.

The kitchen smells of German chocolate cake and vanilla pudding as Zenith and I prepare the ingredients for the kitty litter cake. Eric boils water for the instant gelatin and plucks grapes and dumps canned cherries and tiny marshmallows in a bowl. His phone beeps. He wipes his hands on a towel and mops the sweat from his brow before checking the message. Deep furrows line his forehead and his mouth pinches into a frown.

"What's wrong?" I ask, trying to peek over his shoulder to read the message.

Eric shows me the screen. The text message from Lori reads, "False labor. Stopping by to sample fare."

My voice trembles with panic. "She knows where we live?"

Zenith reminds us. "We're listed in the school directory."

"Oh, right." I glance at Eric, but he seems unfazed. He fills the brain mold with gelatin and grapes and cherries and marshmallows, and sets it in the refrigerator. Then he wets a sponge and wipes the counters.

Zenith and I finish melting Tootsie rolls in the microwave. We quickly shape and bury them into the pudding-soaked cake and sprinkle crushed vanilla cookies over everything until we have achieved the desired effect of a real kitty litter box complete with a pooper scooper.

The doorbell rings.

"I'll get it!" Zenith says, running for the door.

I look around for Eric, but he has disappeared.

Lori's scratchy voice fills the room before she enters. "I'm sure Gina mentioned it," she says to Zenith. My eyes widen with surprise. Lori does not look like the svelte waif I remember from last school year. She still has thin limbs and long pale hair, but the rest of her body looks like a bloated whale dressed in a very purple dress with low black heels. Her icy blue stare takes in our tiny kitchen in our tiny house, and finally settles on the kitty liter cake on the dining room table.

"You have a cat?" she asks.

"No," Zenith says. "That's kitty litter cake for the party. Try some." She heaps a scoop on a plate and hands it to Lori with a fork.

Lori sniffs the cake and pokes at it with her fork. "It smells like chocolate," she says.

"German chocolate," Zenith says. "And white cake and vanilla pudding, too!"

"What's this?" Lori pokes at a melted Tootsie roll and wrinkles her nose.

"Hell-ooh," a voice interrupts. We all turn around. A ghastly clown with blood-covered fangs lurks in the doorway. I scream. Zenith laughs. Lori drops her plate of kitty litter cake and grabs her stomach. "I think I'm going to faint," she says. I grab her by the elbow and help her settle on a chair.

Eric removes the mask and chuckles. "Did I scare you into real labor?"

Lori pants. "I—can't—believe—you."

Eric laughs. "Fear Bozo or die."

Lori continues panting.

Eric sets the mask on another chair and cleans up the cake from the floor. I pick up the plate. Luckily, there are no chips or fractures.

Zenith comes around the table and touches Lori's arm. "I'm sorry my daddy scared you," she says.

Lori smiles briefly at Zenith. "No worries. I should have been expecting no less, since it is Halloween soon." She glowers at Eric. "You aren't wearing that to the party, are you?"

"Why not? All the kids will be dressed up."

"You'll scare them," she says.

"Ah, come on. Don't be a party pooper. It'll be fun." He makes her another plate of kitty litter cake. "Eat up."

Lori shakes her head. "I thought you had everything under control. But you haven't even hired a staff to help you."

"I don't need a staff," Eric says. "I have other parents bringing things, too. You need to relax and stop worrying about everything being perfect. It's all about how much fun the kids have, not how perfect everything needs to be."

Lori clutches her abdomen and winces. "I think I might be having contractions." She waves her hand toward her purse and Zenith hands it to her. She rummages around and takes out a cell phone and calls for someone to come to the door. "I think I should go back to the hospital. I've had a terrible fright." She snaps the phone shut and glowers at Eric again. "I wish I would have known this is how you handle things."

The doorbell rings and Eric leaves to answer it. A man in a suit comes into the kitchen to help Lori stand up.

"Is that your husband?" Zenith asks.

Lori shakes her head. "No, honey, my husband works on the weekends to provide for his family. This gentleman is my driver, Mr. Scott."

Zenith stares at Mr. Scott in his smart suit. His blank stare matches Zenith's blank face. I wonder what she's thinking.

After they leave, Eric bolts the door and laughs. "Did you see Lori's face?"

I giggle. "She did look a bit pale."

"Absolutely ghostly," Eric says.

We both laugh.

"That's not nice," Zenith says. "You scared her." Zenith places the mask over her head and growls. "I'm going to scare you, Daddy!" She chases Eric down the hallway. Their mock screams grow faint and slowly disappear.

On Monday morning, I stand in front of the bathroom mirror in my terry cloth robe and comb the knots out of my damp hair. I grab a can of mousse from the shelf and shake it vigorously. The bathroom door creaks. I jump with fear and accidentally hit my jaw with the can of mousse. My mouth swells with pain.

"Oh, no, Mommy, what happened?" Zenith stares up at me with wide, frightened eyes. "I didn't mean to scare you. I just wanted to say goodbye before you left for work."

My lower lip throbs with pain.

"Don't worry, Mommy. I'll take care of you." Zenith disappears.

While she's gone, I turn toward the mirror. A dribble of blood leaks from a cut on the upper lip. My lower lip puffs into a purplish-red bump. It looks like I've been punched by a very angry person with a good right hook, only that person happens to be me.

Shit. I look like shit.

Oh, God, I'm sorry. I didn't mean to swear.

A few moments later, Zenith returns with an ice pack wrapped in a towel. I tilt my chin and press the ice pack firmly against my lower lip.

"What time is it?" I mumble.

Zenith leaves the room and returns, breathless and worried. "Seven-fifteen."

I motion for her to step aside. "I'm going to be late if I don't leave now."

"But your lip is still bleeding."

Eric wanders into the bathroom and squints at me. "What happened to your face?"

"Zenith scared me and I hit my mouth with a can of mousse."

Eric's gaze flickers from my mouth to the can of mousse. He erupts into a fit of giggles.

"It's not funny," I say. "I'm in pain and I'm bleeding and I have to leave for work."

"Here, Mommy." Zenith opens the drawer beside the sink and removes a Band-Aid. "Wear this till the bleeding stops."

Oh, no. I will not show up to work sporting a Band-Aid as an accessory.

"Can you both move?" Eric asks. "I have to go pee."

I step into the hallway with Zenith.

"Let me help you, Mommy."

Reluctantly, I bend down so Zenith can place the Band-Aid sideways on my lip so I can speak.

"You look like a broken Barbie," she says.

I glance at my watch. "Shit, I'm going to be late," I say. "Sorry, honey. Mommy didn't mean to swear."

"You'll make it, if you take your car."

"Yes, honey, I would, but I don't have money for gas."

Zenith darts across the hall to her bedroom and returns with her fists full of bills and change. "Now you do."

I remember all the times I've sacrificed my gas money so Zenith can have money to do fun things with Mindi. Now, my daughter is sacrificing her allowance to help me.

"Thanks, sweetheart." I try to kiss her, but the Band-Aid tugs tight against my skin. I pat her head instead. "Love you."

"I love you more," she says.

I arrive at the bank and notice that Frank's Porsche is not parked in the reserved slot near the front. I hustle inside, brew a strong pot of coffee, and sit at my desk waiting for Frank to show up for our mandatory meeting.

A moment later, my phone rings.

"Good morning, Beverly Mael," I say, as brightly as I can.

"You're late," Frank says.

I frown. The Band-Aid tugs against my skin. Oh, shit, I forgot to remove it. I tug it loose as I talk. "Where are you calling from?"

"My office. I biked to work this morning. Where else would I be at seven-thirty on a Monday morning?"

Home, I think. Like most people would be.

"I'll be right out," Frank says.

I hang up the phone and dispose of the Band-Aid and take a sip of coffee before it gets lukewarm. Frank strolls out of his office and sits on the edge of my desk and clasps his hands in his lap and starts to talk. Everything he says, he has already repeated several times over the last two weeks. I start to wonder if there might be another reason why he wanted me to come to work earlier than everyone else.

Frank stops talking and glances at me. His dark eyes focus on my mouth. "Did someone hurt you?" he asks.

I touch my face and shake my head. "I just had a little accident," I say, "with a can of mousse."

Frank's mouth creases with concern. He lowers his voice confidentially. "You know, Bev, I care about you a lot. Not just as an employee, but as a friend. If someone is hurting you, you can tell me. Your secret is safe with me."

I can't believe it. He thinks I'm being beaten by Eric. But how can I make him think otherwise?

"Really, it was an accident," I stammer. "I was getting ready for work and my daughter came into the bathroom and startled me. I hit my face with the can of mousse and busted my lip. That's the truth."

Frank reaches out and strokes my cheek. His skin is rough and warm. My face tingles at the unexpected touch. His fingers trace the outline of my jaw. My whole body feels unexpectedly warm. He gazes at me with soft, compassionate eyes. My heartbeat stutters in my chest. He pinches my chin and tilts my head up toward the fluorescent lights. I hold my breath, afraid to move.

He releases my chin and says, "If he ever touches you again, you let me know and I will take care of it."

"But he didn't—"

"Of course, he didn't," Frank says in a patronizing voice. "But if *anyone* hurts you, please find the strength to tell me and I promise you that person will never harm you again."

What's he going to do? I wonder. Hire a hit man? Or kill the person himself?

A cold shiver runs down my spine. I grab the warm cup of coffee and take a couple of gulps. But the tension remains between us. It's an odd sensation, since it's entirely personal.

I try to think of a way to direct the conversation back to work, but Frank speaks first.

"It was great seeing you at the art reception," he says. "By the way, I thought you might like to know that I bought one of your paintings."

"Which one?" I ask.

"The heart one. It spoke to me in a way the others didn't. But they were all good. You'll get the money after the fair ends this week. And I'll get the painting."

I should be happy I sold one of my paintings, but a bolt of indignation darts through me. Frank bought *Heart Cage*, which I painted for Eric. If I had known Frank would want to buy the painting, I would have told Eric to make it ridiculously unaffordable.

Frank flashes a crooked smile. "Is that the first painting you've sold?"

I want to lie, tell him I've sold a dozen others, but I don't feel like putting up a charade. "Yes, it's my first."

Frank winks. "It won't be your last. Soon you won't even need to be working here anymore."

I laugh. My mouth hurts. I frown. It hurts some more. What am I going to have to do for the next few days while this thing heals? Walk around with a blank expression on my face?

"I'm serious," Frank says. "You're very talented."

I glance away and shuffle some papers on my desk. "Thank you," I whisper.

"Don't be so shy about it," Frank says. "Be bold. Make a statement. That's what your art does. It talks to people in ways you can't talk to them."

He stands up and motions for me to follow him into his office, but I don't want to follow him. I want to go home.

"Is something wrong?" Frank asks.

I stare at him for a long moment. He's wearing his sunglasses on his head as usual and the dark blazer with the T-shirt and tight jeans and expensive dress shoes, but something is different about him. And then it hits me—he's relaxed and happy at work, not miserable like he was at the art reception. It's almost as if he works to escape home. Sadness fills me.

"Are you sure you're all right?" Frank asks. "You look like you're going to cry."

"I'm fine," I say, gathering my sketchbook and a pen. I follow him into the office and shut the door and sit down across the desk from him.

Frank hands me a set of spreadsheets. "These are the final figures from World."

I compare the numbers on the spreadsheets with the preliminary numbers given to us when we made our offer to purchase World Bank. "Where did these numbers come from?"

"The last audit," Frank says.

The audited figures are exactly seven million dollars less than the preliminary figures. I rifle through my notes and pull out the article in the newspaper reporting World's stellar third quarter earnings. The numbers quoted in the article match the numbers in the preliminary report. The seven million dollars represent a portion of World's profit. "Do you have the original Excel spreadsheets?" I ask.

Frank frowns. "I already forwarded them to you. Why?"

I gather my notes and stand up. "Because I'm going to get to the bottom of this."

At my desk, I pull up the spreadsheets and toggle back and forth between them, trying to figure out what is wrong. I know from working with Romi that it is not uncommon for preliminary figures to differ from final figures, sometimes even drastically.

When I get stuck, I take out my sketchbook and start to doodle. I draw whatever comes to mind. Circles, stars, and squares fill the page. When I tire of drawing, I return to the spreadsheets. The equations are the same; the balances total perfectly.

Maybe something has shifted between the different accounts. Frank said it's not unusual for banks to redistribute their portfolio when they're in trouble. But what would World redistribute? And how would I go about proving it?

Maybe something is hidden in the spreadsheet. Like one of those Easter eggs Eric always talks about programmers putting in their programs. Would a bank do that?

Hmm. I glance at the clock. Eric should still be home. I pick up the phone and call him.

"Hello," he says.

"It's me," I say. "I have a quick question."

He laughs. "Nothing with you is quick."

"Really, Eric, I'm serious." I lower my voice, although I am the only one around. "Do you know if you can hide something in an Excel spreadsheet?"

"Sure, you can hide all kinds of things. Columns and rows can disappear. You can even lock it so no one knows what is missing. Why?"

Hmm. I know I shouldn't do this, but I don't feel like I have a choice. My curiosity is too strong. "Do you know how to break into a locked Excel spreadsheet?"

Eric chuckles. "I wrote a program for that."

"Can I use it?"

"What are you breaking into? I don't want to get prosecuted for aiding a bank in unlawful activity."

"But you did that stunt with PG&E."

"That's different. I was doing it. If I give it to you, you'll be doing it. You don't have the skills I have."

"I can follow directions."

There is a pregnant silence.

"Okay," Eric says. "I'll e-mail it to you. Download it to your desktop and run it as a utility. I'll type up instructions in a separate e-mail that I'll send to your personal account that I want you to check from your phone. Understand?"

I try to smile, but my mouth hurts. "Yes, I've got it."

***

A few minutes later, I find it. The hidden column. The seven million dollars.

I stand up too quickly, knocking over my half-empty cup of coffee. I mop up the mess with a few napkins stashed in the top drawer of my desk. I snatch the spreadsheets from the printer and throw open Frank's door.

"I found what World is hiding," I say, waving the spreadsheets triumphantly in the air.

Frank swings his legs off the desk, sits up, and turns down the volume of Van Halen singing, "Runnin' with the Devil." He extends his hand. "Let me see."

I walk over to him and place the spreadsheets on the desk. I stand beside him, bending down closely to point out the hidden column marked, *Loan Loss Reserve*, in big bold letters. I don't know what it is, or what it means, but I found it.

"Well, well, well." Frank whistles soft and low. "Look at that jackpot."

My face hurts from smiling. I want to turn up the music and grab Frank's hand and dance around the room until we're both breathless. But I don't. I stand solemnly beside him, my finger pointing at the column of numbers totaling seven million dollars.

"Thanks for finding this, babe," Frank says.

I remove my finger from the spreadsheet. "What does it mean?"

Frank sighs. "It means World inflated their profits for the third quarter to encourage investors to bid up their stocks. And it worked."

Wow. Something was wrong. And I found it. Maybe that means the deal is over and the stress will be gone, and I can go home at five o'clock and spend time with my family. "So, are we going to cancel our purchase?"

Frank studies the numbers and slowly shakes his head. "No, we're not. But it does give us leverage if Buddy decides to play games with us."

"Why would he do that?" I ask.

"Pride," Frank says. "There's always pride before the fall."

***

Eric greets me at the front door when I get home. "How's my little hacker wife?" he asks. "Find anything good?"

I kick off my shoes and sink down on the sofa. Zenith curls up next to me and rests her head against my chest. "I missed you, Mommy," she says.

I kiss her forehead. "I missed you, too."

Eric sits on the edge of the sofa. "Tell me, tell me, tell me," he says.

The rush of excitement I felt this morning upon unlocking the spreadsheet has not diminished, although I am exhausted from working a twelve-hour day. "I found seven million dollars World was trying to pass off as profits."

Eric jumps up. "Now that's what I'm talking about," he says, giving me a high five.

A flush of pride warms my body. The skin around my mouth feels sore and swollen when I smile.

"That's why I stay up late tinkering with the computer," Eric says. "It's amazing how much power you can have if you know what you're doing."

Zenith lifts her head from my chest. "How did you find the money?" she asks.

I gaze into her brown eyes and feel a twinge of guilt. Hacking into a locked Excel spreadsheet might not be as dramatic as turning off the city's lights, but it is still illegal and immoral. It doesn't matter that I uncovered the truth. I went about it the wrong way.

Sorry, God, I'm becoming like Eric. I guess that means I can't judge him anymore, right?

Zenith looks at me expectantly. The room grows silent, and all I can hear is our soft breathing.

"I found it by knowing where to look," I say, slowly. "Just like when you and Mindi play Hide and Seek. You always find her, right?"

Zenith's eyes sparkle. "That's because I know all the good hiding places," she says.

"And Mommy knows where all the numbers are supposed to go," I tell her. "So, if they aren't there, I have to start looking for them."

Zenith frowns. "Where do numbers hide?"

"They don't hide," I tell her. "People hide them."

After we have said our family prayers, I tuck Zenith into bed. She clasps me tightly around the neck and whispers, "Remember, you promised you'd paint us matching ladybug nails for Halloween."

I hug her tightly. She smells of my Victoria's Secret shampoo and conditioner and her bubble gum toothpaste. "I haven't forgotten, dear. We'll do it tomorrow after dinner. I promise."

She sinks down into her pillows and smiles. She looks just like her father with her wide, dark eyes and pale skin and big hands. I stroke a thick brown curl away from her forehead and wonder if it's too late to have another child. It's not like Eric and I haven't tried over the years; it's more like Eric and I haven't cared one way or another whether we expanded our family or not. We never took family planning very seriously like other couples. We just kind of drifted and said if it's meant to be, it will happen. When it didn't happen, we just figured it was God's will.

But now, I wonder if we've given too much of our power to God and saved too little for ourselves. I wonder if it's too late to take some of that power back. How different would our lives look if we shaped them to suit ourselves, instead of relying solely on prayer?

Zenith reaches out for my hand and squeezes my fingers. "You look sad, Mommy."

"I'm just tired," I tell her.

"I keep praying you won't have to work anymore."

"I know, dear. I've prayed for that, too. But maybe it's time to pray for something else."

"Like what?" Zenith asks.

I kneel down beside her bed. "Acceptance," I say.

"Buddy called," Frank says as soon as I sit down at my desk the next day. "He wants to meet us for lunch tomorrow. Wrap this whole deal up before month's end. What do you think? Need to leave early to go shopping? Get your hair and nails done? You want to look spiffy tomorrow. It's the big day!"

Frank dances a jig beside my desk. I'm afraid to get near him, because I might catch fire from the heat of his excitement. He seems to be glowing from within. His eyes sparkle and his mouth twitches with anticipation. He slaps a drum roll on my desk and twirls around and punches the air with his fists. "Woo-hoo! World will be ours!"

I tug the necklace as if trying to loosen a noose, but it doesn't budge. My skin feels cold with fear. What if Buddy doesn't have good news for us? What if he prefers to deliver bad news in person at a crowded restaurant so he can watch Frank squirm with disappointment? Fear eventually dissolves into disappointment as I realize I will be unable to attend Zenith's Halloween party. Even worse, I will have to tell her I cannot paint my nails to match hers. Frank said I have to be polished and professional.

Even though I have no intention of going shopping for new clothes, I take Frank's suggestion and leave for the rest of the day. I wait until I'm in my car to call Eric on my cell phone and tell him the news.

"I wish I had known sooner. I'm stuck at Mike's right now."

"What are you doing at Mike's?"

"I'll tell you later. Why don't you go home and relax? Paint a little. You haven't painted since the Harvest Fair."

I hang up with Eric and call Vi. Her voice mail picks up instantly. That means she's with clients. "Hey, it's me," I say. "I have the day off and wanted to know if you want to grab lunch. I'll be at home, painting. If you get this message, call me."

At least my car is fixed. And I have extra money in our checking account from my big raise. I could splurge on a makeover, if I wanted. But as I pull out of the parking lot, I glimpse the cool Fall sunlight glinting off the big windows of Vine Valley Bank and feel the impulse to save, save, save to buy my freedom back anyway I can.

***

"But Mommy, you promised!" Zenith wails when I tell her I cannot paint our nails in matching ladybug colors because of my meeting with Buddy from World Bank tomorrow.

Eric moves around the kitchen clanging pots and pans while talking on the phone.

I sit down at the kitchen table beside Zenith. "I wish I could, honey," I tell her. "But, I have to look professional for work, and that means no ladybugs."

She sniffs back tears, trying to be brave, and for a moment, I feel like I need to be brave, too. So much has happened so quickly, I don't recognize who I am anymore.

I remember Romi's warning, "I just hope you know what you're getting into, and that you're doing it for the right reasons." What started out as a job to pay the bills has transformed into an accidental ambition to prove myself to the world, when all I really need to do is prove myself to me.

I glance over at the painting I started today called *Taking over the World*. It is my attempt to imitate Marc Andre Souza's *Social Media Blizzard* by combining mixed media to make a statement beyond my little world. I used the newspaper clipping about World Bank for the sky and crumpled one dollar bills into a make-shift papier-mâché globe, and tied it all together with forest green paint. I didn't like my first attempt, so I scraped the paint from the canvas and tried again. It took forever, and it's still not right. But I am pretty pleased with my efforts to go beyond my comfort zone and try something new.

Zenith stares at her fingers. "I guess I don't have to have my nails painted either," she says.

My heart is broken, as broken as it was when Vi told me she could not rearrange her schedule so we could meet for lunch today. I reach over and grab my daughter's hands and hold them for a moment. Someday, Zenith will care to spend more time with her friends than with me. And, at the rate things are going, I'll still have to work.

My gaze returns to my painting. I remember how hard it was to get the right consistency of paint, how I had to scrape and paint again and again. Scrape and paint, scrape and paint.

That's it.

I release Zenith's hands. "A promise is a promise," I say. "Let's paint some matching nails."

"Really?" Zenith stares at me dubiously. "But what about your meeting?"

"You're more important than work," I tell her. What she doesn't know is I am going to remove the nail polish before my meeting with Buddy tomorrow. Before I come home, I'll paint them again. No one will know my little secret.

Zenith wraps her arms around my neck and says, "You're the best mommy in the world!"

Chapter 25

In the morning, I wear the red and black Liz Claiborne dress suit I borrowed and never returned from Vi and my standard black heels. I tuck the Vine Valley Bank necklace into a zippered pocket in my purse. I will put it on once I'm at the office so I don't upset Eric or Frank. I pack a bottle of nail polish remover, a handful of cotton balls, red and black nail polish, and a teeny tiny makeup brush. I rub a bit of scented lotion into my hands, brush my hair until it is glossy, and dust a bit of powder on my face to set my makeup.

Eric whistles at me. "Wow! You're hot!"

Zenith twirls around in her ladybug outfit. "We look the same. Except I have antenna and you don't."

I hope I don't look too much like a ladybug. The black dots on my red nails are a bit conspicuous, but I enjoyed painting them with Zenith. I still remember the way she bit her lower lip as I dipped the teeny tiny makeup brush into the black polish and painted each dot into an elaborate pattern on each nail. "It looks so real," she said, admiring my handiwork. I feel a pang of longing in my chest as I bend down to kiss Zenith's cheek. "Have fun at the Halloween party."

"Don't worry. I'll stream it," Eric says. "If you're busy wheeling and dealing, you can catch the video on YouTube afterward." He kisses me. "Don't worry. I'll send you a link."

I hate to go, but I have to. Reluctantly, I hug them both to me. "I wish I could be with you."

"We do, too, Mommy," Zenith says.

***

Frank doesn't bother with formalities. He swaggers out of his office and slaps a drum roll on my desk. "We're leaving at a quarter to ten, babe."

I stop typing and glance at my watch. Yikes. We're leaving in five minutes.

As soon as Frank disappears, I throw my sketchbook in my purse and slip into the restroom. I place my manicure set on the counter by the sink and douse a cotton ball with acetone and scrub my nails vigorously. Red paint smears over my cuticles and the tips of my fingers. I discard the soiled cotton ball for a clean one. It's harder to get this stuff off than I thought it would be.

The door swings open and Romi steps inside. She frowns at my reflection. "What are you doing?"

"Getting rid of a ladybug manicure," I say. "I promised my daughter I would paint us matching nails, but I have that luncheon to go to and I want to look professional."

Romi's frown deepens. "What's your daughter going to say when you get home?"

I flash a smile. "She won't know the difference. I'm going to paint them again."

Romi shakes her head and steps into a stall.

I rinse my hands and notice the tips of my fingers look like raw meat. I dry my hands with paper towels and grab another cotton ball.

"Beverly Mael, please come to the front desk," Jim says over the intercom. "Beverly Mael, please come to the front desk immediately."

Oh, no. I spill the nail polish remover on the counter. It splashes on the tile floor. I grab some paper towels and mop up the mess.

Romi flushes the toilet and joins me at the sink. "Need help?"

I toss the paper towels into the waste basket and rinse my hands. "No, I'll be fine."

"Remember to breathe," Romi says.

I run down the hallway in my heels. Frank leans against the counter in the reception area. When he sees me, he lowers his sunglasses over his eyes. "What happened?"

"I had to use the restroom. I didn't want you to have to make a special stop for me."

Bright autumn sunlight glints off the cars. Frank holds open the passenger's door to the Porsche. "We're going to be stopping anyway. I need an extra tall mocha before our luncheon." He's dressed in a black suit, white shirt, and a flashy silver tie. When he bends down to close the door, I catch a whiff of L'Homme by Yves Saint Laurent. Mmm. I bet it would smell even better on Eric. It's more subtle and sensual than the cheap cologne he wears. Hmm. Maybe I should buy him some for Christmas.

Frank drives fast, as usual. I take out the necklace from my purse and clasp it around my neck. The medallion seems dull from oxidation, but it probably just needs a little silver polish. I try not to fiddle with the necklace or my purse handles, or tap my feet to Def Leppard singing, "Love Bites." I gaze out the window. The sky burnishes with a silvery blue haze. Heat pulses out of the vents. I feel like a puddle of nerves against the buttery seats. At a stop light, I remove my jacket and fold it neatly in my lap. My arms seem as fragile as porcelain against the bright crimson of my dress. I splay my fingers. Not too bad, I think. You can't even tell they were painted, unless you look really, really hard.

Frank stares straight ahead and drums his hands on the steering wheel when he isn't busy shifting gears. I can't see his eyes behind his sunglasses. I don't know where we are going and I don't bother to ask.

Finally, we stop at a café. Frank releases his seatbelt and lowers his sunglasses. "Want anything?" he asks.

My heart hammers in my chest. God, he's so attractive. I want to kiss him. No, no, no, I think. That can't be right. He's my boss. I can't have a crush on my boss. I twist my hands in my lap and glance away. It's stress, I think. I've been under an incredible amount of pressure. That's it.

"I don't want anything," I lie.

"Sure?"

I can change my mind. I can tell him how I want to run my fingers through his wavy hair while his hands trace circles against my lower back. I hold my breath against the intoxicating scent of his expensive cologne and try to think of something else. Anything else.

Frank continues to gaze at me with his intense hazel eyes.

I open my mouth to speak, but nothing comes out. I feel absolutely foolish.

"Okay, then, I'll be right back." Frank slips out of the Porsche. I watch his hurried swagger. He pauses to hold the door open for a woman. Just before he steps inside, he turns toward me and winks. A flicker of desire whips through me. I instantly glance away. I don't know why I'm feeling this way. I fumble in my purse and grab my phone, risking a quick call to Vi. She picks up on the first ring.

"Vi Patel," she says.

"It's me," I whisper, although I am the only one in the car.

"My, you're calling early. What's going on? Aren't you supposed to be at work?"

"I *am* at work. I'm in my boss' Porsche, waiting for him to buy a mocha." I shift in my seat, trying to see where Frank is through the double glass doors, but I only glimpse a crowd of people standing in line. My palms sweat. I have to say what I want to say as quickly as I can before he steps outside and I have to hang up with Vi. "I don't know what's wrong with me, but I think—I mean—I wonder—is it normal to feel a little magnetism toward another man?"

"Are you talking about your boss?" Vi asks.

"Umm," I pause. "If I tell you the truth, you can't tell Eric."

"Of course I would never tell Eric. You know I'm practiced in confidentiality."

I close my eyes and exhale. "Yes, it's my boss." A wave of relief washes over me. "I mean, sometimes I feel absolutely nothing, but every now and then I get a little physical jolt and I wonder if it means anything."

"It's normal to be attracted to other men, even when you're happily married," Vi explains. "You can't do anything about how you feel. You can only choose whether or not to act on your feelings. Understand?"

"Umm. Maybe." I have no idea what she is saying. Does that mean it's okay to feel vibrantly alive whenever Frank pays me a compliment or winks at me or calls me babe, as long as I don't jump his bones or get too attached to his flirtatious attention?

Vi sighs. "I'm not your psychologist. I'm your friend. And as your friend, I'm telling you to be careful. Don't disclose any personal information to your boss and don't let him disclose any personal information to you. Keep it professional. And when things get too heavy, take a break from each other if you can." She pauses. "It's a little difficult to do when you're in a moving vehicle. Where are you going with him anyway?"

"If you listened to me, you would know," I say.

There is a thoughtful pause. "Is this about World Bank?"

"We're going to buy them out." I lower my voice. "That's also confidential."

"No problem. I won't leak the news to the press."

Frank approaches the double glass doors.

I duck my head, hoping he won't see me talking on the phone. "I have to go. He's coming back."

"Good luck," Vi says. "Remember—don't do anything you wouldn't do in front of Eric. That's what I tell all my clients. It keeps them faithful."

I hang up, toss the phone in my purse, and straighten my skirt. Frank hands me a bag full of mini-muffins. "Try one," he says. "I'm going back inside for my mocha."

I'm too nervous to eat. I cup the warm paper bag in my hands and stare anxiously at the double glass doors. Frank pushes his way out of the café. His hands cradle a huge mocha. He slips inside and closes the door. "What did you think of the muffins?"

I shrug. "They're fine."

He holds the mocha in one hand and rifles through the paper bag with the other. "You didn't even try one." He frowns. "Don't tell me you're on a diet."

"No, I'm just too nervous to eat." I wave at my skirt. "And I'm naturally clumsy. I might spoil my dress."

"Here." Frank removes a mini-muffin and holds it up to my lips. "Take a bite."

No way is he going to feed me. That's too personal, isn't it? What would Eric say if he saw?

"C'mon, open up." Frank nudges the muffin against my closed lips. "Just one bite."

This is embarrassing. He's not going to stop until I take a nibble. Reluctantly I open my mouth and bite down. Warm cinnamon and apple flavor bursts into my mouth. "Mmm. It's good," I say, between chews.

He flashes a crooked smile and pops the rest of the muffin in his mouth. I watch his lips twist as he chews. My face burns. Oh, God, please keep my thoughts chaste, I silently pray. When that doesn't work, I glance away, knotting my hands into fists.

"My wife won't let me eat this stuff," Frank says. "She thinks it will kill me. But I can't take another bowl of steel cut oats. That stuff makes me want to gag." He slurps his mocha and munches on another muffin. "What she doesn't know won't hurt her, right?" He winks at me.

I slightly nod. Keep it professional, I remind myself. Think of something else to talk about, something not personal. Okay. I can focus on the luncheon with Buddy. I turn toward Frank and smile. "Are we giving Buddy a formal presentation?"

Frank laughs. "I don't need to. I brought you."

He *brought* me. "What is that supposed to mean?"

"Buddy likes you. He'll do anything for you. That's just the kind of guy he is."

My whole body chills. A moment of silence stretches between us until it feels like we are sitting on opposite sides of a deep ravine. Frank finishes the bag of muffins and stuffs in into his empty cup. "Did I say something wrong?" he asks.

All these weeks, I thought my mind really mattered to Frank. I thought he saw some hidden potential behind the beautiful body. But he was just plotting to use my pretty face to lure World Bank into his overambitious hands.

I'm not smart. I'm not talented.

I'm just bait.

Eric and Vi were right.

I feel so stupid.

Stupid, stupid, stupid.

Hot tears prick my eyes. Don't cry, I tell myself. You'll ruin your mascara. Think good thoughts. Everything will be all right.

Frank fiddles with the MP3 player, going from song to song, until he finally settles on "Master of Puppets" by Metallica. He taps on the steering wheel and bobs his head to the beat. I sink back against my seat, wishing I could disappear. I check my watch. It's only eleven o'clock. We have another hour till we make it to Spa County. I take out my phone and search for a message from Eric, hoping he has already posted pictures on Facebook. But my inbox is empty. I browse the Internet, hoping to find something to distract me.

A few minutes later, Frank lowers the volume on the stereo and glances over at me. "Tell me what's wrong, babe."

I drop my phone into my purse and stare out the window. Rows and rows of vineyards snake up the mountainside. Clouds scuttle across the gray sky. "Nothing's wrong," I lie.

"Are you nervous about seeing Buddy?" Frank asks.

I feel trapped in a steel box with no way out. If I tell Frank the truth, then I may lose my job. If I tell Frank a lie, he will eventually pester me until I tell him the truth. Either way, I lose.

"Buddy doesn't respect me," I say. "And neither do you. I thought you kept giving me extra work to do because you thought I had potential. But now I know it was only a sham. You need me to get World Bank. That's all I am. A means to an end."

Frank frowns. "That's very Machiavellian of you," he says. "I take it you know who Machiavelli is."

"Sure I know him," I lie. I don't want Frank to know I'm ignorant. He already thinks I'm stupid.

"I do respect you," Frank says. "I gave you more responsibility, because I knew you could handle it. And I gave you a raise, because you earned it. That's how I treat all of my employees."

"Then why did you make that comment about not needing to make a formal presentation to Buddy, because you're bringing me?"

Frank slaps the steering wheel. "You're mistaking Buddy's chauvinism with me. I don't think you're going to close the deal. Buddy thinks you're going to close the deal." Frank shakes his head. "Sometimes, Bev, you have to use all of your assets. You're not just smart. You're attractive. Smart, attractive women are the most powerful people on the planet. That's why I don't need a formal presentation."

"Because I'm a smart, attractive woman," I echo numbly.

My phone beeps with a message. Eric must have posted some pictures of the Halloween party online.

But I don't care about the party right now. Right now, I don't care about anything.

Frank's voice is thick and hoarse. "I'm sorry you feel I've used you," he says. "I had no intention of making you feel that way. And I understand if you don't want to come to the luncheon. I'd be willing to drop you off to do some window shopping while I meet with Buddy if that would make you feel more comfortable."

Does he really feel that way, or is it just another ploy to get me to comply with his true intentions?

For a long while, neither one of us speaks. I grab my phone and scroll through the pictures Eric sent. The whole classroom is decorated like a haunted castle with glow-in-the-dark cobwebs and big fuzzy black spiders and a drawbridge that operates by remote control. Everyone is dressed up and having fun. I wish I was there, not here.

I wish I could type Eric a message about what I'm going through with my boss, but I know it would just upset him, which would just upset me. Instead, I type an innocuous message. "Thanks for the pics. Looks like you're having lots of fun. Big meeting almost here. Wish me luck." I close my phone and clasp my hands tightly in my lap and wait for Eric's response.

Several minutes pass. I check my phone. Nothing.

Oh, well. Eric is probably busy with the Halloween party. I'm surprised he even had time to post the pictures.

I toss my phone in my purse and close my eyes.

Chapter 26

"Shall I drop you off?" Frank asks.

The Porsche idles at a four-way stop near a row of shops. Artist's Grotto, Biquor Books, Christy's Candles, and Davina's Delights line one side of the street. Ann Taylor, White House Black Market, Talbot's, and See's Candy line the other side of the street. Women dressed in expensive casual wear go in and out of the shops. They look a lot like the mothers in Zenith's classroom. The women I used to hang out with when I was a stay-at-home mother, a world away from where I am now.

I shake my head wistfully. "I'll go to the luncheon with you." I have to accept my circumstances, I think. I have to take responsibility for where I am in my life, even if that means making sacrifices.

Frank lowers his sunglasses and peers over the lenses at me. "Are you sure? I don't want you to feel uncomfortable."

I shrug. "It doesn't matter how I feel," I say. "I have a job to do."

Frank flashes that sexy crooked smile, the one that makes my heart flutter and my knees wobbly. "You've got moxie, babe. That's one of the many things I admire about you."

This time, I absorb the compliment without getting flushed and giddy like a school girl. I guess Vi's right. I can be attracted to another man and not act on it.

The valet opens the passenger door and helps me out of the Porsche. Frank meets me on the sidewalk. We are outside the Warm

Out of Balance

Water Restaurant and Hotel where we stood a month ago. So much has changed.

The air is nippy and smells of fresh rain, although the pavement is no longer wet. Frank places his hand on my lower back and escorts me up the stairs to the grand entrance. I let him hold the door open for me and I step inside, feeling the warm air envelope me like a hug. The thick carpets sink beneath my heels. As we approach the restaurant, a waft of pumpkin pie and roasted coffee greets us.

"I think we should have a plan, if Buddy stalls," I say.

"He won't stall," Frank says. "But if he does, it's your job to distract him while I make the appropriate calls."

Great. My job is to distract Buddy. What does Frank expect me to do? Shake my breasts in the guy's face?

A waiter dressed in an immaculate tuxedo leads us across the dining room.

Buddy is waiting for us at a table by the full-length window overlooking the street. "Hey, hey, hey, it's my favorite people." Buddy stands up and kisses my cheek. He shakes Frank's hand and pulls back a chair so I can sit next to him. Frank takes the other seat beside me. I glance from Buddy's chubby face to Frank's chiseled face and wonder what I am supposed to say.

Buddy leans close to me, gazing down at my dress, and talks to Frank. "I know you're expecting me to present you with the signed contract, but I have a proposition."

I shift in my seat and tug my jacket over my chest.

Frank eyes Buddy suspiciously. "Our offer is final."

Buddy gazes at the buttons on my jacket. "I think you'll agree that in light of our recent stock prices, we are worth much more than your initial offer." Buddy removes a set of papers from his briefcase. "Here's our counteroffer."

I glance over Frank's shoulder. I don't believe it. Buddy wants twice the amount of money we agreed to.

From inside my purse, my cell phone rings. I jolt upright and reach for the strap hung over the back of the chair. No one calls me during the day. Yes, I get text messages from Eric and Vi, but if it's important, they know to call me at work.

By the time I find my cell phone, it has stopped ringing. I check the number and frown. I don't recognize it.

Must be a wrong number, I decide.

The same waiter returns to our table with a bottle of champagne and three flutes.

Did Buddy order champagne? Isn't that a little premature? What does Buddy think, anyway? That we're going to crumple and take his offer without consulting with our Board of Directors first?

The waiter pours the champagne into flutes and hands them to us. "Are you ready to order?"

I groan. How long is this buyout going to take? One more month? Or six months? It better not take a year. I don't think I can handle working this hard for that long.

Buddy orders the steak and fries, and Frank orders the salmon and grilled vegetables. I haven't even glanced at the menu. I'm still puzzled over Buddy's counteroffer.

My phone beeps with a message.

Why would a person who reached a wrong number leave a message?

I close my phone and tuck it back into my purse.

Frank leans close to me and whispers, "Turn off your phone. Or put it on vibrate. That's what I do. You need to stay focused, okay?"

I reach back into my purse and turn off my phone. A teeny-tiny part of me wonders who called.

The waiter lists today's specials. I stare blankly at him.

Frank leans over and whispers, "You seemed to enjoy the lobster salad last time."

"Yes, I did. I think I'll have that."

The waiter collects our menus and leaves.

Buddy lifts his glass for a toast. "To Vine Valley Bank, the best and soon-to-be biggest bank west of the Rockies."

Frank does not touch his glass of champagne. He hands Buddy the contract. "Not for this price."

Buddy refuses to take it. "I'm sure your Board of Directors will agree it's an equitable offer."

Frank frowns and pats his chest. He removes his cell phone from his breast pocket and peers at the screen. "Why is the bank calling?" he mutters. "They know I'm in a meeting." He turns off the phone and slips it back into his pocket.

The waiter delivers a bread basket. I twist my napkin in my lap and stare at my glass of champagne. The bubbles pop against the surface. *Oh, please, God, let these negotiations end today. I promise I won't complain about working, if I can only go back to working 9 to 5, at least through the holidays. I miss my family. I miss my time. I miss who I used to be.*

I glance over at Frank, hoping he can read my thoughts. But Frank is not looking at me. He's looking at Buddy.

Buddy sets down his glass of champagne and reaches for a piece of bread, which he butters on both sides.

Frank taps his fingers against the table. "Your stock prices are inflated as the result of your last press release, which, by the way, is inaccurate."

Buddy chuckles. "I can't interpret our numbers for the press. That's their job. My job is to see we make a profit."

Frank nods. "Even if that profit comes from—"

"Pardon me, Mr. Martin." The waiter stands with his hands clasped in front of him. His brown eyes are solemn with the weight of bad news. "The hotel concierge has informed me there is a call from Jim Harris at Vine Valley Bank. He is trying to reach Beverly Mael. He says it is urgent."

I glance from the waiter to Frank. My heart patters in my chest. "May I?"

Frank's frown deepens. "How urgent?" he asks the waiter.

The waiter shrugs his broad shoulders. "Mr. Harris said it was a family emergency."

Family emergency? I knock over my chair when I stand up. My purse tumbles to the floor and the two bottles of nail polish roll across the carpet under the table. I bend down on my hands and knees and gather them up with shaking hands.

Frank reaches for my arm and briefly squeezes it. "Are you going to be all right?"

I ignore his question and follow the waiter out of the restaurant. I hustle across the lobby beneath the twinkling lights of the gigantic chandelier. My legs feel like rubber, and my breath sputters like I've just finished running up a hill.

At the registration counter, a young woman with a high pony tail and a swath of bright red lipstick hands me the phone.

"Hello, this is Bev," I say.

"Beverly, it's Jim. I've been trying to reach you. A woman called from the police station. She said your husband has been brought in for questioning and someone needs to pick up your daughter from school. I tried the emergency phone numbers listed in your HR file, but I could not reach anyone. Is there someone else I should call?"

Why is Eric being questioned by the police? Why didn't Vi return Jim's call?

I glance at the golden clock behind the registration counter. It's twelve-thirty. If I leave now, I can make it in time to pick Zenith up from school. "Don't worry, Jim. I'll handle it. Thanks for calling."

I hand the phone to the concierge and return to the restaurant. So much for reverse psychology. I should have prayed to St. Jude for a miracle instead. My heels sink into the plush carpet, muffling the angry steps of frustration I feel. Why is Eric at the police station? Is it about the prank with PG&E? Or his connection with Black Magic? Or something else, which I know absolutely nothing about?

Frank and Buddy are bantering back and forth when I arrive. The entrees have been served. Frank glances up at me briefly, taking in the shock and horror that must be splattered across my face.

"I need to go," I say.

"What happened?" Frank asks.

"I need to pick up my daughter from school."

Buddy clears his throat.

"What about your sitter?" Frank asks.

"I don't have one. My husband picks her up."

"Where's your husband?"

I blink my eyes rapidly, trying to stem the threat of tears. My voice cracks. "He's being questioned by police."

Frank pulls back my chair and pats the seat. "Sit down. Have some lunch. I'll get you back in time to pick up your daughter from school. I promise."

I glance at the fresh romaine lettuce covered with croutons and lemon slices and big chunks of lobster and shake my head. How can I eat when my husband is at the police station and no one else can pick up my daughter from school?

Buddy clears his throat again. "Let her go, Frank. She doesn't need to be here."

Frank reaches for my hand. His skin is warm and comforting against my chilly palm. "Please, stay. We haven't finished talking."

Talking? That's what he calls this cat and mouse game he's playing with Buddy?

Buddy chuckles. "She doesn't care about business. She cares about her family. Let her go pick up her kid and bail her husband out of jail. We can finish our discussion when she's gone."

Did Buddy just say I don't care about business? I have not worked so hard for so long to have someone insult me like that.

I spin around and narrow my eyes at Buddy. He immediately focuses his attention on my chest, but I'm too angry to care anymore. "You're wrong. I do care. In fact, I care more about this deal than I should," I say. "I've given up time I could have spent with my family so I could pour over your financials and sort out this mess. I even told Frank we shouldn't buy your bank. It would be better for us to let you go to the Feds and let them conduct a full investigation into your creative accounting methods. But Frank insisted on giving you an opportunity to retire peacefully with your pension. If I were you, I'd sign the initial offer with no questions asked."

Buddy's beady black eyes move from my chest to my eyes. His mouth parts slightly, but he seems too stunned to say a word.

I turn toward Frank. "I have to go. I've already stayed too long."

Buddy waves his hands. "Wait." He lifts his briefcase and sets it on the table and removes a set of papers. He hands them to me. "Here's the initial offer signed and approved by the Board of Directors."

My fingers close over the document. I flip through the pages, scan the wording, and run my finger over the signatures in blue ink. I turn around and offer the papers to Frank.

We've just bought World Bank.

Chapter 27

Okay. I admit it. I'm thrilled we purchased World Bank.
But I'm also a teeny-tiny bit worried about Eric.
Frank shifts into high gear. We barrel down the two-lane highway, trying to get back to Vine Valley before two-thirty.
"You were fabulous today," Frank says.
"It wasn't exactly Business 101," I say. "The delivery could have been better."
"But you earned Buddy's respect. That's a first."
I lean back against the buttery leather seat and listen to the voicemail message on my phone. Detective Joanna Speers says her partner is interviewing Eric in a case they are investigating. "We don't know how long it is going to take," Detective Speers says, "so Eric wanted you to know he will need you to pick up Zenith from school. I'll try your office and leave a message there, too."
That's it. No details about what they are investigating, or what type of questions Eric is being asked, or if he'll be home in time for dinner, or locked up in a jail cell overnight.
"Any news?" Frank asks.
"Nothing," I say, flipping my cell phone shut. I gaze out at the vineyards and the clouds scuttling in the gray-blue sky and say a little prayer.
"Do you want me to drop you off at the bank or the school?" he asks.
Well, it would be faster if he dropped me off at the school, but there's no room for Zenith in the Porsche. "The bank," I say.

"You know I'm going to miss my two o'clock mocha," Frank says.

I smile in spite of the worry knotting my stomach. "You'll be missing a lot more, once the baby arrives."

Frank winces, as if I have scalded him with hot water. "Don't remind me. I think part of the reason why I've been so consumed with World Bank is so I don't have to think about how scared I am of becoming a father."

"I think I understand your fear." I reach for my sketchbook and turn to a blank page and begin to draw as I talk. "I was scared to go to work. I liked being a housewife just as much as you like being President and CEO. It's what we feel we were born to do. Then someone we love throws a monkey wrench in our lives and we get out of balance. But what I've learned is you don't have to let it crush your spirit. Sure, I'd rather be window shopping with a bunch of gossiping housewives, but telling Buddy off today felt so much more rewarding."

Frank laughs. "Did you see how quickly he looked up into your eyes? I thought he might have suffered whiplash."

My smile broadens. "It did feel good to prove to him that I am more than my looks." I stare at my sketch. A mountain full of vineyards slopes down to a flowing river. I tuck the pencil in the spiral spine and close the sketchbook. "You know you have a lot more to offer than your business skills. You have a heart full of love and a soul full of music. Sharing that with your wife and your future children will be more fulfilling than any bank acquisition, if you just stop fighting against it."

A moment of silence hugs us.

"Thanks, babe." Frank reaches over and pats the back of my hand. "We make a great team."

A warm feeling of satisfaction spreads throughout my body. "Yes, we do."

We pull into Vine Valley Bank's parking lot at a quarter after two. Frank parks beside my old Escort but leaves the engine idling. I can't believe Frank kept his promise and got me back on time to pick up my daughter. I reach across the seat and awkwardly wrap my arms around him.

"Thank you for everything."

"Anytime," Frank says, patting my back. "If you need to take tomorrow off, just leave me a message, okay?"

I hesitate a moment before releasing him. God, he smells good. I definitely need to get Eric some of that cologne.

From the car's stereo speakers, Queen sings, "We Are the Champions."

A tiny thrill shoots through me as I remember the victory of my little speech with Buddy that led to the purchase of World Bank.

I am smart.

I am talented.

I gather my belongings and open the door. I glimpse my reflection in the wide windows of Vine Valley Bank. I look as polished and professional as Romi, even as I slip into my car to get my daughter from school.

Frank waits until I've started my car before he drives out of the parking lot to get his afternoon mocha.

I follow him to the first light. He turns left, and I turn right.

I remember one of the first things Frank told me. If I can balance a checkbook, I can balance a general ledger.

He was right. But there is one thing I would like to add.

If I can balance a general ledger, I can balance my life.

The playground is crowded with children dressed in Halloween costumes. I spot a ladybug with black antennae standing by the slide.

"Zenith!" I run across the parking lot, dodging cars and minivans. I wrap my arms around her. She smells like cupcakes. I kiss her cheek. Her skin is sticky with sugar. "Tell me what happened."

Zenith squirms out of my arms. Her face glows with animation. "Daddy planned the best Halloween party ever! Even Gina's mom showed up. She was so surprised, she wet her pants! The janitor had to come mop it up. Gina's mom kept screaming, 'My babies! I'm going to have my babies!' It was hilarious! Daddy was filming it until the police showed up."

"At school?" I sink down on my knees. Gravel cuts through my nylons. I can't believe my daughter watched her father get hauled off by the police.

"Uh-huh." Zenith nods. "The principal showed them where we were. They said they've been looking for Daddy for a long time."

Damn, it's that PG&E scandal all over again, I think.

Sorry, God, for swearing.

Zenith glances around. "Where is Daddy?"

I take a deep breath and sigh. "He's still with the police."

When I called the police station on the ride back from Spa County, Detective Speers said the talks were confidential. All of my questions were deflected. Even my daughter doesn't know what's going on, and she was present when the police arrived.

I stand up and take Zenith's hand. A brisk wind sweeps across the playground, scattering leaves across the pavement. I shiver. Zenith squeezes my hand and asks, "What happened to your nails?"

Oh, shit. How could I have forgotten?

Sorry, God, sorry, sorry, sorry.

My face flushes with shame. My brilliant plan backfired. Sure, it would have worked, if I had remembered. But who remembers their nails when their husband is talking with police in an investigation, and their boss is driving 100 miles per hour on the freeway? Seriously. Only superficial women with nothing better to do would remember. Or maybe mothers who think only of their children. But I don't fit into either category, do I?

What will I tell Zenith?

I bite my lower lip as I unlock the door to the Escort. Maybe I should just tell her the truth.

When we are both inside the car, I turn to her and say, "Mommy had an important meeting today and she wanted to look polished and professional, so she removed her nail polish before the meeting. But I wanted to be a ladybug for you tonight, so I brought my nail polish with me to paint my nails again. Only I forgot. I'm sorry."

Zenith gazes at me with her wide brown eyes. "Do you have to go back to work?"

I shake my head. "Not today."

"Then you can paint them when we get home."

I reach across and hug her. "You're so smart," I say.

She kisses me with her sugary lips. "That's because I'm just like you."

Chapter 28

After dinner and trick or treating, I tuck Zenith into bed and say our evening prayers. Eric is still not home. I have not tried calling his cell phone. For all I know, the police might have confiscated it.

"…and God bless Mommy and Daddy, Mindi and Ms. Patel and Mr. Norris, Grandma and Grandpa Daniels, and everyone we meet," Zenith prays.

I kneel beside Zenith's bed and try to focus, but I can't. All my thoughts circle back to Eric and his computer antics. Was it the practical joke he played on PG&E that alerted the police, or was it his online chat with a member of Black Magic? Why did God tell him to approach Black Magic if nothing good was going to come of it? Why?

"Mommy, it's your turn to tell God your special intentions," Zenith says.

I glance at my daughter. She seems so peaceful lying in bed with her hands clasped over her chest. I wish I could stop worrying. Sure, there are moments when I am happy and carefree and relaxed. But the rest of the time, I am plagued by doubts.

"Thank you, God, for Vine Valley Bank purchasing World Bank today. Thank you for Zenith and me having a great time trick or treating." I lower my voice. "Please help Daddy to come home soon. Please help him to stay out of trouble, and please help us to understand and forgive him when he does not. Please help Mommy to be the best mommy for Zenith and the best wife for Daddy and the best employee for Frank. And please help the economy to get better and for there to be enough food, love, and peace throughout the world. Amen."

"You forgot something," Zenith says.

"What?" I ask.

"Thank you, God, for Gina's mom finally having her babies."

I snicker.

That's something Eric would have said.

At midnight, the lock in the front door jiggles. I leap out of bed and run down the hallway just as Eric opens the door and steps inside. I can't see his face at first. His head is bent and his shoulders are slumped as he flicks on the light and closes the door. I rush over to him. He lifts his head and gazes into my eyes. I expect him to look worried or troubled or upset, but his eyes gleam and his mouth curls into a smile.

He's happy. Why is he happy?

"What happened?" I ask. "I was so worried."

Eric places his hands on my shoulders and gently squeezes them. "Didn't they tell you?"

I shake my head. "No one told me anything."

Eric pulls me close for a hug. He smells of coffee and cigarettes, although he prefers Mountain Dew and chewing gum. He is still wearing his clown costume minus the mask. The baggy parachute pants crackle like cellophane against my flannel pajamas. His breath is warm and gentle against my ear. "I asked them to tell you."

I pull away. "Who are you talking about? The police? They didn't say anything to me."

Eric's stomach grumbles. "What did you guys have for dinner?" He goes into the kitchen.

"I ordered a pizza." Oh, God, I must be a bad mother. Eric would have started the crock pot before leaving for the day. I didn't even think about dinner until it was too late to make anything.

"Did you save any for me?" Eric doesn't say anything about my negligence.

"There are a few pieces left." My relief about my mothering skills evaporates. Fear coils in the pit of my stomach. Why did the police want to talk to him? What did he say? I trail him into the kitchen. "Aren't you going to tell me what happened?"

Eric fills a tea kettle with water. He sets two mugs on the table along with two bags of chamomile tea. I sit down at the table and watch him move around the kitchen with the grace of a dancer. My hands are shaking and my heart is thumping and my thoughts are racing. Why won't he just say what he has to say, instead of dragging the whole thing out?

"Are you hungry?" Eric asks.

I shake my head. "I'm too anxious to eat. I just want to know what happened."

Eric finds the leftover pizza and brings it to the table. The tea kettle whimpers, and Eric fills our mugs with steaming water. I dunk the bag up and down, up and down. I bite my lower lip to keep from jabbering. After twelve years of marriage, I know the less I say, the sooner Eric will talk.

Eric finishes the pizza and cups his mug of tea with both of his large hands. He stares off into space for a long while and I notice the long lashes fringing his dark eyes, the eyes I fell in love with so many years ago.

My heart clenches like a fist in my chest. I don't know why I am so worried. I can't protect him. And I know, deep down, he doesn't want me to. I'm so nervous; I'm shredding a tissue from the box on the table just like I did the day Eric told me he had been laid-off. I knew he was really fired for fooling around with the computer systems at work. Since the day he lost his job, our lives have been turned upside down. Nothing has been the same. I sadly realize I've never forgiven him, and I'm secretly afraid it's going to happen all over again. I don't know if I'm strong enough to take a second round.

Eric's warm hand covers my hand and the tissue I am shredding. "I'm sorry they didn't tell you," he begins. "But I couldn't leave the meeting to tell you myself. It was very intense, something I never imagined happening, not in my wildest dreams. Having Mike there even made it seem more surreal."

I slowly lift my eyes to take in his expression. There are furrows on his forehead and beads of sweat gleaming on his bald head. He's scared to talk to me. He's frightened to tell me the truth.

I swallow, hoping to clear the tightness at the back of my throat.

Eric squeezes my hand and continues. "The police tracked me down when the FBI contacted them about a little incident regarding Black Magic. Apparently, someone from Black Magic used my metasploit to launch an attack against a government agency. But the person didn't modify the code correctly, so it triggered a series of alerts." He must see the confusion on my face, because he pats my hand and says, "It's complicated. That's why the FBI wanted to talk to me. They wanted me to explain how the program worked, why I sent it to Black Magic. Mike was there to represent me. Then the FBI contacted the NSA. We had a telephone conference that lasted two hours. To make a long story short, the representative at NSA wants to test my firewall, see if it's as impenetrable as I say it is. Mike drafted a contract that was reviewed by their attorneys and faxed back signed. NSA is going to beta test my product. I'll make any changes they suggest. If they like the final release, they will purchase licenses. I'll have a steady income at last."

I stare at him, unable to think or speak.

"You know what the NSA is?" Eric asks.

I nod, remembering. It's the National Security Agency in Maryland. It's the government agency Eric wanted to work for when he first graduated from college, because he said he would be defending our nation against cyber attacks. But he never got a call back on his resume. He ended up continuing to do what he had already done.

"Isn't it great the way God works?" Eric asks.

But I'm not thinking about God or the NSA. I'm thinking about the coils of relief uncurling throughout my body. My hands have stopped shredding tissue. My heartbeat has returned to normal and my breathing has, too. Eric is not in trouble. He hasn't worked himself into another corner. He hasn't turned our lives upside down, but somehow managed to turn our lives right side up.

"They don't want to prosecute you for writing the metasploit?" I ask. "They don't know about your prank with PG&E?"

Eric chuckles. "I'm pretty damn good. I don't play with fire, if I know I'm going to get burned. You know that."

"Do I?" I ask, narrowing my gaze.

He stares at me seriously. "Listen, Bev, I'm sorry about losing my job. I know I made a mistake, but I really think it was a blessing in disguise. I like the freedom of working for myself. I like exploring things without someone breathing down my neck about deadlines or budgets. And I like being home with Zenith. I've really gotten to know her better being with her this past year. It's something I'll always cherish. But I also know it's been hard on you going back to work full-time after being home for so long. The shock on your face every day used to make my heart break. I didn't want to say anything, because I didn't want to make it worse. You're such a worry wart. I didn't want you to worry about me worrying about you. But I miss seeing you happy. I think Zenith misses seeing you happy, too. I don't know how long it is going to take to perfect the product, or if I can even get enough licenses sold to generate enough income to bring you home from work, but I'll do everything I can to try. I want to see you happy again. We all do."

I glance down at our hands tangled together with the tissue. "You know, the reason why I was so upset about working was because no one took me seriously except Frank. We bought World Bank today, and it was because of something I said to Buddy. I finally got the respect I deserve. It felt good. Really good." I release Eric's hand. "I like working. I never thought I would, but I do."

Eric sips his tea in silence. "What did you say?"

I smile. "I told Buddy to take our original offer or he would face an investigation for creative accounting."

Eric chuckles. "Was this before or after you discovered I was being questioned by the police?"

I blush. "After."

Eric laughs. "You were worried about me, weren't you?"

"That's not why I said it."

"Go ahead and pretend it had nothing to do with me, but I know the truth. You thought I was in trouble. You always think I'm going to get into trouble." Eric winks.

I bite my lower lip. "Well, even if I was thinking of you, I was talking to Buddy."

Eric reaches over, pulls me into his arms, and kisses me. "Congratulations."

His lips taste of pepperoni and chamomile tea. "Congratulations to you, too," I whisper. Now I have an excuse to buy that expensive cologne before Christmas.

Eric kisses me again. His lips linger against my mouth, and my whole body softens. When he finally releases me, I gaze up into his face and see the admiration he has for me reflected in his eyes.

About the Author

Angela Lam Turpin is the author of *Legs* and *Blood Moon Rising*. She balances her time between raising her family, working in real estate and finance, and writing her next novel.